Christmas

Magic, Mystery, and Mirth

Other Books by Debbie Viguié

<u>Witch Hunt</u>

The Thirteenth Sacrifice
The Last Grave
Circle of Blood

<u>Retold Fairy Tales</u>

Midnight Pearls
Scarlet Moon
Violet Eyes

Christmas Magic, Mystery, and Mirth

By Debbie Viguié

Published by Big Pink Bow

Christmas Magic, Mystery and Mirth

Copyright © 2014 by Debbie Viguié

ISBN-13: 978-0-9906971-2-1

Published by Big Pink Bow

www.bigpinkbow.com

Dedicated to all my family and friends.

I love you very much.

TABLE OF CONTENTS

Christmas Pearls

Once upon a time in the Kingdom
of Aster the prince was married to
a young woman who was not what
she appeared. Though the union
was a happy one the young woman
was sad because she felt herself
alone, a stranger in a strange land.
Her tears were so numerous that
they threatened to drown the land
and all the people. Then something
occurred to change all of it. The
young woman gained a true friend
and what happened next was a
Christmas miracle that would be
remembered for generations
untold.

The Kingdom of Aster, Once Upon a Time

It was two weeks before Christmas and the skies were weeping with an abandon that none in the kingdom had ever before witnessed. The rain had started with the dawn and by midday the streets of the village below the castle were flooded. The waters ran off toward the sea, but the sea itself was angry and dark and the waves were encroaching further and further onto the land until the people murmured that the sea king was trying to reclaim that which had been taken from him, a young mermaid who had walked out of the sea many months before to claim the heart of their beloved prince.

As the rain pressed on the villagers sought shelter in their homes. There was one solitary figure, though, who walked the waterlogged streets, head and arms bare. She scarcely felt the water as it sluiced over her body. In the back of her mind she sensed it as a vague, comforting feeling, a memory of a life that was lost.

Faye should have been happy, but she wasn't. The last several months had been wonderful, crazy, and oh so much more. She had found her true love, been changed from a mermaid to a human woman, and married. She had also left behind her brother and the rest of her family to embrace this strange new world.

James, her husband, was the prince of Aster. Which, of course, made her the princess. It was hard to be the princess of a land where everything was so strange, though. It was bad enough that she didn't understand any of the customs and she constantly had to be educated about everything that pertained to this human life she was now living. Being a princess, though, put distance between her and everyone else. The result was that outside of her husband she didn't have any real friends.

And as she stared in bewilderment at the huge tree that was now standing in the middle of the village she realized that what she wanted most was a friend. The day before people had been singing and dancing around the tree when it had been erected. Castle servants had placed fruit and sweets on the tree much to the delight of a group of kids who had gathered wide-eyed to watch. She supposed once the rain stopped it would all need to be replaced.

She had been told that this was the happiest time of the human year which was why she felt bewildered by the sorrow and misery that seemed to be weighing down her heart. Even her nearly perpetual smile had been turned into a frown the last couple of days.

Every window she passed had lights shining brightly in it, far more than actually needed to illuminate the rooms they were in. She was told that this was another tradition of the season, the chasing away of the night and the celebration of the truest of lights. It should have made her feel warm inside, but somehow the cold just seemed to creep further into her bones.

She walked to the edge of the sea and stared toward the horizon, hoping in vain that she might catch sight of a familiar face or fin or tail. It seemed the creatures of the sea that had once been her friends no longer knew her for they never showed themselves anymore.

When she had grown tired of looking she made her way back to the castle. No sooner had she entered than one of her maids saw her, and clucking disapproval, hurried her upstairs to her chamber and helped her remove her wet garments. The woman left with them and Faye slowly began to dress. The feeling of clothes was one she still was not entirely used to. Aside from being constrictive the fabric itself chafed against her skin.

Her skin was so much more fragile than it had once been. As a mermaid her tail had been covered in scales, tough yet flexible, protecting her many dangers. What had passed for skin on her upper half had been thicker, more impenetrable though more translucent.

"I can't wait to share our first Christmas together," a soft voice said behind her.

She turned and saw her husband James smiling at her. She forced herself to smile back.

"Feeling a bit overwhelmed?" he asked.

She nodded. She could never hide her emotions from him.

He reached out to take her hand. "If you want to cancel the feast tonight we can."

She shook her head. "It would be rude. The Earl of Lauton and his wife have traveled far to be here and they deserve a proper reception."

"William is a very interesting fellow. His wife is unconventional. I've been told that before their marriage she worked as a blacksmith," James said with a twinkle in his eye. "Something tells me the two of you will get along well."

Faye shook her head as she couldn't help but wonder which of them would be more out of her element.

The sound of the rain pounding down outside drew his eyes to the window. He frowned. "I've never seen it rain so hard in all my years."

"Maybe it will never stop raining," Faye mused.

"That's impossible," he said.

Looking out the window Faye wasn't so sure about that.

James gave her a quick kiss. "I'll see you downstairs shortly?" he asked.

"Yes."

A few minutes later Faye descended to the main floor wearing a new green gown that James loved because he thought that with the gold accents it looked very festive. She hoped that it would help hide her mood from her guests.

Faye hated feeling this way. Normally she was full of energy and joy. These dark feelings didn't sit well with her, but try as she might she was struggling to shed them. She at least managed to force a smile into place before entering the great hall.

William was already there talking with their guests. She noted that the other woman was wearing a blood red dress. Together they would look doubly festive.

"Earl William, Lady Ruth, this is my wife, Princess Faye," James said, drawing her forward to meet the others.

"Welcome to our home," Faye said as William bowed and Ruth curtsied. She did notice that the motion was awkward for Ruth. She looked to be about the same age as Faye herself. Her hands were strong and covered in a number of tiny scars and calluses. James had mentioned that Ruth had once been a blacksmith and looking at her hands it was easy to believe that it was true. "Will you be staying with us through Christmas?" she asked.

"No, your highness, we will be returning home before then," William said, "in order to spend the time with our families."

Families. Maybe the problem was that she was missing hers too keenly at present to be joyful. Still she didn't think that a quick trip under the sea, even if such a thing were possible, would fix what was wrong with her.

Ruth smiled at her, but it didn't reach her eyes. Sorrow was lurking there and Faye was startled to see it. She had thought herself the only sad person in all the world at this time of year. Impulsively she reached out and took Ruth's roughened hand in her own.

"Merry Christmas to you," she said, realizing that it was the first time she'd actually said the words to anyone.

"Merry Christmas to you as well, your highness," Ruth said.

"Please, you must call me Faye."

Next to her she could see James grinning. She took Ruth's arm and walked with her toward the table. "I hear that you had an interesting life before finding your Earl," Faye said.

She could feel the other girl stiffen next to her and she squeezed her arm. "Before I met my prince I wasn't even human," Faye confided. "I'll tell you my story if you'll tell me yours. I warn you, though, my story involves a curse."

"So does mine," Ruth said, sounding genuinely surprised.

"Then we should get along swimmingly."

Throughout dinner Ruth told Faye her story and the princess found herself quite taken out of her own troubles as she listened to Ruth's tale.

"Show me the scars where the wolf attacked you," she pleaded at one point.

All around them servants and feasters halted their own activities to look at her in shock. Faye realized that her request was somehow inappropriate. Even James looked a little shocked.

Faye bit her lip, but Ruth reached out her hand and put it on Faye's arm. "I would be happy to show you after dinner," she said earnestly. "You won't believe how ugly they are."

"And yet beautiful because they bind the two of you together," Faye said, indicating Ruth and William.

William flushed, clearly embarrassed. Clearly she had said something wrong.

"That is a wonderful way of looking at it," Ruth said, giving her a dazzling smile that put Faye again at ease.

After dinner they hurried to Faye's sitting chamber. Once they were in there alone Ruth hiked up her skirts to reveal crisscross scars up and down her legs.

"Wow, that must have been so painful," Faye muttered as she gingerly touched one of them.

"It was. It was hard to walk afterward."

"And yet you not only walked, but you also took up a hammer and became a blacksmith."

Ruth shrugged. "Someone had to help my father since my brother left for the crusades."

"And since you became William's wife?"

"I'm not supposed to do that stuff anymore. I'm supposed to be an Earl's wife, whatever that is. Honestly, I feel like a fish out of water most of the time."

Faye clapped her hands at the phrase. "Yes, exactly!"

"Only you really are a fish out of water," Ruth said with a laugh.

One of the servants entered. "May I bring you some tea?" she asked.

"No, we are fine at the moment," Faye said.

"Is there anything else I may bring you?"

"Well, I'd ask you to have a couple of horses saddled so I could show Ruth the town, but that's not a good idea with all the rain," Faye said.

Actually she wanted to show Ruth the ocean and the spot on the beach where she had emerged from it for the first time.

"Your highness, the rain stopped nearly an hour ago. I believe the roads are still quite treacherous, but if you were careful you might be able to take the horses out."

Faye turned eagerly to Ruth who nodded. She turned back to the servant. "Tell the stable master to expect us shortly," she instructed.

Faye still wasn't entirely comfortable on horseback, preferring to walk where and when she could even though it still felt odd to have legs. She wouldn't put Ruth through walking that far through mud and muck, though.

A few minutes later they were riding out of the castle. The clouds had cleared from the sky and bright stars twinkled down at them as they rode to the beach. While they rode Faye told Ruth her story and was gratified at the excitement the other girl showed in hearing it.

When they finally made it to the beach they stared out to sea. It was nice having someone to share with, someone who saw herself as an outsider as much as Faye did.

"I've never had a close friend before," Ruth said after a while.

"It is nice, isn't it?" Faye asked. "I just know we're going to be the best of friends forever."

"Even our husbands seem to be getting along which is nice. William can be a bit intense for some people."

"He was a werewolf for most of his life, how could he be anything else?"

"True."

"How many days journey is it between our homes?" Faye asked.

"Four by carriage, shorter by horseback," Ruth said.

"That is not so bad. You can come visit often."

"And we would be honored to have you visit us," Ruth said.

"What fun! I'd love to see your home and meet your family. I only wish you could meet mine."

The thought touched her with sorrow for a moment.

"Did you feel that?" Ruth asked.

"What?"

"I could have sworn I felt a drop of water on my cheek."

"Maybe it was spray from the ocean."

"I'm sure my grandmother would love to meet you, a real live mermaid!"

"Former mermaid."

"I wonder what your children will look like?" Ruth mused.

"I've often wondered." Faye had a sudden thought and she laughed out loud. "Wouldn't it be amazing if we all had children and our children married your children?"

"It would be a miracle," Ruth said, her voice suddenly strained.

"What's wrong?" Faye asked.

"It seems that William and I are unable to have children."

She could hear the other girl's pain and it hurt her terribly. It also burst the happy little future she'd been envisioning where they were all family.

"Are you sure?"

"We've been married two years. My grandmother has worked some potions for us, but nothing."

She could hear Ruth's pain even more sharply in her voice.

"I'm so sorry," she said.

Raindrops began to fall from the sky and she glanced up. She could still see the stars and she wondered how that could be when clouds should be covering them. It was just one more thing she didn't understand.

It wasn't fair that Ruth should suffer so.

"Maybe we should head back to the castle," Ruth suggested.

"Sorry, you're probably right," Faye said with a sigh.

"What's wrong?" Ruth asked.

"I feel bad for you."

"It's okay. Who knows, maybe we will find that miracle. After all people tell me that two years isn't so long that I should give up all hope."

"That's true," Faye said.

The rain suddenly eased off.

They turned their horses' heads back toward the castle and began riding. The rain almost stopped, leaving just a faint drizzle.

A terrible thought gripped her out of the blue. "You don't think you're inability to have children has anything to do with the curse that William was under, do you?"

"I have to admit I had wondered the same thing myself."

"You don't think James and I will have problems, since I was once a mermaid?" Faye asked. She couldn't imagine how empty their lives would be without children and she hung her head in grief at the thought.

The skies opened up and water poured down over them, hard and pounding.

"We have to seek shelter!" Ruth shouted.

She kicked her horse into a run and Faye did the same. The storm lashed out harder and harder as they raced back to the safety of the castle.

Faye felt her horse stumble, sliding slightly in the mud, and it unseated her. The beast scrabbled to get his footing and just as he gained it she lost her seat entirely and went sliding off his back and into a mud puddle.

Ruth stopped her horse, jumped off and ran back to her. "Are you okay?" she shouted.

It was hard to hear her over the roar of the wind and the rain.

Faye nodded and tried to stand up. Her feet slipped out from under her and she fell back down into the mud, splashing some all over Ruth.

To her surprise Ruth started laughing. She reached down and tried to help Faye stand and a moment later they were both on the ground in the mud. Ruth just started laughing harder and the sound was contagious.

Faye snickered.

"We look like a couple of very fine ladies now," Ruth said.

Faye laughed out loud as she imagined the scowling faces that would greet them when they returned to the castle in this state.

And just like that the rain stopped.

Ruth looked up quickly, a puzzled expression on her face. Then she looked back at Faye.

"Faye, how were you feeling earlier today, before we met?"

"Sad, why?"

"Something strange is going on with this weather. It feels like magic to me. It's almost like it's tied to your moods. When you're sad it rains. When you're happy it stops. That makes no sense, though. I just don't see what could cause that."

"I do," Faye said with sudden understanding.

The pearl necklace that she was wearing, the one her brother's wife had given her, was magic. The necklace had allowed her to permanently change from being a mermaid to a human girl. It had been able to give her the desire of her heart. Maybe it was somehow now reflecting the emotions of her heart.

"Quick, say something depressing," Faye said.

"I have nightmares sometimes that I do have a baby, but it's a wolf instead of a human."

And just like that Faye had the horrible thought that she might give birth to a mermaid and have to send her child away to live with her family.

The rain came pouring down harder than ever.

"Say something funny!"

"When we get back to the castle we should make mud angels on the floor of the great hall by lying down and moving our arms up and down like wings."

The image was so absurd that Faye burst out laughing.

And just like that the rain stopped.

"You're right! It is tied to my moods!" she said.

"So, any chance on keeping you cheerful until we can get inside?" Ruth asked.

"I think we'd better try. Now if only we could get out of this mud pit we've found ourselves in that will be half the battle won."

They did a great more slipping and sliding before they could stand up and make it to their horse. Faye tried three times to get on before deciding to walk. Ruth rode slowly beside her leading the other horse.

By the time they made it to the castle both their husbands were frantic with worry. And she and Ruth promptly proceeded to make the mud angels Ruth had described on the floor much to the horror of the servants.

The next morning while James and William conducted some business, Faye found Ruth in the ballroom admiring some of the Christmas decorations. Faye drew Ruth to a couch where they were able to sit down.

"I have a Christmas present for you," Faye said.

"I didn't get you anything," Ruth said with a frown.

"That's okay. I hadn't planned on giving you anything, but when I woke up this morning I'd had a dream and I knew that this was the right thing to do."

She held out the pearl necklace. "I want you to have this."

Ruth's eyes widened. "I couldn't take that. It's part of your family's legacy, your story!"

"And as my first true friend, I want you to have it," Faye said, folding it into the other girl's hand. "It has magic. It can show you your destiny, and it can even help you achieve it."

As she said it, she could feel the pearl growing warm. Ruth gave a little gasp, clearly feeling it, too.

"What do you feel?" Faye asked.

Ruth shook her head, her eyes wide in wonder. "I don't just feel it, I see it."

"Then what do you see?"

"A child, a boy. It's my son, and he's human, not a wolf. And he's playing with a little girl who looks just like you."

Faye felt happy tears filling her eyes. "See, we are going to be family after all."

Ruth hugged her and Faye felt warm deep inside.

Two days later when Ruth and William left the castle Faye and James stood, watching them go.

"Are you okay?" he asked.

"Yes," she said, smiling. "I know we'll see them again soon."

"I'm glad that you seem much happier than you were."

She turned to him and gave him a kiss. "I don't have to be embarrassed anymore when I don't understand things. Ruth is having a hard time fitting into her new world and she was human to begin with. If she can do it, so can I. I will learn all that I can and consider it a privilege and not a burden."

"I like hearing that," he said with a smile. "Ready to enjoy your first Christmas?"

"I've already started, and I think I understand one of the most important things about Christmas."

"What is that?" he asked.

"It is better to give than to receive."

DEBBIE VIGUIÉ

Tex Ravencroft and the Pearl of the Orient

Hong Kong, December 1930

Archaeologist Tex Ravencroft was sitting in
the most elegant night club he'd ever seen staring
down some Chinese gangsters and wondering
how he'd gotten himself into this particular
situation. He shook his head slowly.

When his friend, Nathaniel Grant of the
Smithsonian Institute, had told him that he had an
acquaintance who needed a particular artifact
located and retrieved he should have passed.
Doing things for friends of friends wasn't usually
his style. What could he do, though? When it
came to finding lost antiquities, Nathaniel gave
him more work than anyone else. After this,
though, Nathaniel would owe him.

It turned out the hard part of acquiring the
pearl Nathaniel's friend wanted wasn't finding it,
it was bargaining for it. The pearl in question was
a giant one, black in color, and it hung from a
simple gold chain. The pearl was purported to
have some sort of magic, although Tex didn't
believe in such things.

The pearls origins were shrouded in mystery. What was known, though, was that Marco Polo had it with him when he made his historic journey. It had not returned home with him, though, and in one of his journals he had lamented its loss, saying that it had been stolen from him.

The mob boss across the table from him claimed the pearl had been in his family for centuries. Whether or not one of his ancestors had been the one to take it from Marco was probably unknowable at this point, but it seemed like a safe bet. After discovering the pearl's owner Tex had needed to work hard to find something the man wanted that he was willing to exchange.

It turned out that jade tablet from the Xia Dynasty was what he wanted. It had taken some doing, but Tex had procured the tablet, and now he was hoping to make a peaceful exchange. There was no reason to expect anything else. The tablet, after all, was worth a thousand times what the pearl was.

On the nightclub's stage a Jazz musician who seemed to have been plucked from the heart of New Orleans and somehow found himself on stage in Hong Kong was going to town, playing with abandon. He was doing some fantastic renditions of classic Christmas songs. Tex doubted that many of the patrons would know the original tunes and would appreciate the unique twists the musician was putting on them.

Li, the mob boss, leaned forward slightly as he pulled the pearl out of his coat pocket. "This is precious to my people," he said. "Emperors and peasants alike have bowed to its power. It is a symbol of all China."

"You're telling me there's a real Pearl of the Orient. Who knew?" Tex quipped.

Li didn't smile. "This is not surrendered lightly," he said.

Tex nodded. "No, the cost is high, but I'm able to pay it." He pulled the jade tablet out of his bag and held it up.

Li quickly bowed his head though Tex swiftly realized the gesture of respect was aimed at the tablet and not at him.

"The symbols on the tablet aren't Chinese," Tex noted.

"No," Li said without offering any other explanation.

Whatever the message, it had to be pretty important if someone decided to carve it in jade," Tex said. When he had first laid eyes on the tablet it had excited his curiosity and he was hoping he could extract at least a little information about it out of Li. After all, not only had the man known about it but he had also known approximately where to find it. Of course it had begged the question of why he needed Tex to retrieve it for him. Tex had learned, though, that of all the questions in his business that was one of the ones usually left well enough alone.

Li didn't say anything but his eyes were fixed on the tablet and the look of anticipation on his face was like a child about to receive the present they wanted the most.

If we just get this done and I can get out of here and catch my flight home then we can all have a merry Christmas, Tex thought to himself.

Tex slid the tablet to the middle of the table, keeping one hand on it even as he watched Li closely, waiting to see what move the other man would make.

Li slowly moved both hands to the center of the table. The pearl dangled from his fingers.

Tex reached out and closed the pearl in his hand at the same time that Li touched the jade tablet. "Merry Christmas," he said. Tex lifted his hand from the tablet as he tightened his fingers around the pearl.

And suddenly he had the uncanny realization that the tablet was more important than he could imagine and that he was going to need it one day.

"Christmas isn't coming," Li said. Before Tex could react, Li yanked the tablet from the table and tried to pull the pearl away from Tex.

Startled, Tex still managed to hold onto the pearl even as Li strained to pull it free. The chain snapped in two and the pearl slipped from his fingers, hit the marble floor, and went rolling.

Tex was on the floor, reaching for the pearl by the time that one of Li's bodyguards pulled a gun and fired off a hasty shot in Tex's direction. Tex grabbed his own gun and fired under the table, hitting the man in the leg. He went down with a scream and landed so hard the floor shook and the pearl rolled just beyond Tex's reach.

The nightclub patrons shouted and started running for the exits. More shots were fired as Tex scrabbled across the floor after the pearl. On stage the musician just played on as though he were on the Titanic, seemingly unfazed by the gunfire and the chaos.

A man tripped over Tex, kicking him hard in the ribs as he did so. A woman nearly impaled his left hand with the heel of her shoe as she trampled over it. He blinked against the pain, struggling to keep the pearl in sight. He heard more shots fired and there was sudden blazing pain across the back of his right thigh as a bullet skimmed him.

More people trampled him as their hysteria grew. He set his jaw against the pain and tried to get to his feet. He wasn't going out this way, trampled by a bunch of panicked bystanders.

He made it halfway up before someone careened into him sending him crashing back down onto the floor. He rolled out of the way of a couple more people and found his back against the edge of the stage. There, a foot from him, was the pearl.

His hand closed around the pearl. It grew warm against his skin and suddenly he had an overwhelming sense that there was a heavy weight crushing down on him. His lungs burned as though he couldn't get enough oxygen and he found himself gasping for air. He shoved the pearl in his pocket and when he pulled his hand away he found he could suddenly breathe easy again. There was nothing pressing down on him, no weight seeking to crush him.

He struggled to his feet. The pain in his leg was great, but it would take his weight. He made it half a dozen steps, and then was forcefully spun around by a hand on his shoulder. Li's other bodyguard was standing there, his back to the stage, and murder in his eyes. He leveled his gun at Tex. Just as he was about to fire, though, an instrument case smashed him in the back of the head and the man fell to the floor, out cold.

The musician had stopped playing long enough to pick up his case and knock the guy out.

"Thanks!" Tex shouted to him.

The musician shook his head. "Don't thank me, just take me with you!"

Tex gave him a short nod as the man scrambled off the stage, instrument in one hand, case in the other.

"Let's go," Tex said, heading for the front door.

"No, there's a back way," the man said emphatically.

He had just saved Tex's life so there was no reason not to trust him at this point. He might regret it later, but he nodded and followed the man back behind the stage.

A few quick turns through the building and they exited on a side street. "I have a plane waiting," Tex said as he turned to the left and headed for a larger street where he could hail a taxi.

"Is there room for one more on it?"

"I think we can make do. What's your name?"

"Jefferson."

"Jefferson, call me Tex."

They were able to get a taxi quickly and they were soon on their way to the airstrip where the pilot Tex had hired earlier would be waiting for them. Jefferson quickly put away his instrument and sat, face strained. Tex kept checking out the back window, looking for signs of pursuit. It was possible that in all the chaos they had gotten away clean, but he knew better than to bank on that.

"Do you think we're being followed?" Jefferson asked.

"I don't know," Tex admitted. "We can't take any chances, though. I'm sorry, if you're coming with me we don't have time to swing by your place and pick up anything."

Jefferson lovingly patted his instrument case. "Everything I need is right in here," he said.

"Why'd you save me back there?"

"Two years ago I was playing a club in New Orleans. This Li guy approaches me, says he owns a nightclub in Hong Kong and that he'd been looking for someone like me to play it. He offered me a huge salary, said I'd become famous because nobody there was playing music like mine. It all sounded berries to me, so I took him up on the offer."

"And then something went wrong?"

"I should say. My pappy always used to tell me not to take any wooden nickels, guess I had to learn the hard way. I haven't been his employee, I've been his prisoner. Night after night I've poured my heart out on that stage praying that God would send me a way out."

Tex glanced again out the back of the taxi. "Lucky for me."

"For both, I reckon."

"We'll be there in about two minutes or less. Then we'll be home free."

Suddenly a car shot out of a side street and rammed into the cab, hitting the door next to Tex. The glass shattered, spraying Tex with tiny, needle like shards.

The taxi spun around and they were thrown hard against the side. Shots rang out as the car skidded to a stop.

"Out your side!" Tex yelled to Jefferson.

They got out of the car and ran, keeping the taxi between them and the other car. They made it to the cover of a building and Tex pointed the direction they needed to go to make it to the airstrip.

He was in serious trouble. The guy who had kicked him must have cracked a rib or two because his chest was hurting a lot more than his leg was. There were a dozen small cuts on his face and arms and he blinked hard, trying to get blood out of his one eye which had dripped there from a cut just above it.

"Are you okay?" Jefferson asked.

"No, but I'll be a heck of a lot worse if we don't make it to that plane."

"We'll make it. Do you need to lean on me?"

"No, but let's get moving."

Using the buildings as cover they managed to make it to the airstrip. Fortunately the pilot was true to his word and the plane was already on the tarmac, ready to go.

"We'll be exposed for about ten seconds as we make a run for it," Tex said.

"That's not so long."

"Long enough to get shot. I don't see where we have a choice, though. So, on the count of three. One, two, three!"

They burst from the shadows and began to run toward the plane. The pain intensified and Tex grunted, trying to keep himself together. Just a few more steps. They had reached the plane when the first shot rang out. As Tex helped push Jefferson up into the plane he glanced back and saw the car that had struck the taxi headed their way. A man was hanging out the passenger window firing at them.

The pilot was shouting something, but Tex couldn't hear him over all the noise. He managed to climb in after Jefferson and slam the door shut. He fell into his seat with a grunt of pain as he landed on his shot leg.

The plane was in motion a moment later and within seconds they were airborne. Tex leaned his head back. "I think I might be passing out in a minute," he admitted.

Four days later it was Christmas Eve and Tex was in the hospital back home in Washington D.C. recovering from his various injuries. Nathaniel walked into the room, a small decorated Christmas tree in his hands. He set it up on the table where Tex could see it.

"Thanks," Tex managed to say. He was groggy from all the medication they were giving him.

"Merry Christmas," Nathaniel said.

"I've got a present for you, too. It's in my bag in the closet," Tex said.

Nathaniel opened the closet, inspected the bag, and a moment later was standing there holding the pearl. He had a strange look on his face and Tex wondered what was going through his mind. He decided it was better not to ask.

"My friend will be overjoyed," Nathaniel said at last as he tucked the pearl into his jacket pocket.

"I hope so. It cost me an awful lot."

"Well, hopefully I can make that up to you. I've got another job that requires your expertise."

"If you have another friend-"

"No, this is for me," Nathaniel said, cutting him off. "I'm looking for a particular Hawaiian goblet."

"That's different," Tex admitted.

He winced as he tried to sit up straighter. He was going to be recovering from this particular adventure for a while. "Tell you what, talk to me in a couple of months about looking for your goblet."

"Alright. In the meantime, I'll let you get some rest."

Nathaniel gave him a smile and then left. Tex was dead tired and he wanted nothing more than to sleep for a week. He should write in his journal and record the adventures of the last couple of days. Outside he heard bells ringing. It was midnight. Christmas had come after all.

The Kiss of Christmas Past

*"In whom we have redemption through his blood,
the forgiveness of sins, according to the riches of
his grace;"*

- Ephesians 1:7

Prague, December 23, 1938

The redemption. It's all about the redemption,
Constance thought in awe. She knelt in the
cathedral, feeling the power wash over her. War
was coming. Bloody, horrible war. She knew it,
felt it with every fiber of her being. If she closed
her eyes she could almost see it unfolding before
her, images swirling through her mind. She
prayed for the men who would be fighting, the
families who would be sacrificing. Her own
family had left Prague the week before, heading
to America to live with a cousin there. She was
expected to join them shortly, but she couldn't
shake the feeling that there was something she
was meant to do first.

Her father had told her that her head was full
of dreams. Her mother, though, had squeezed her

hand and told her with her eyes that she understood. The women in her family had a knack for sensing things, particularly when they were needed to pray for something or someone.

The night was closing in around her. Constance loved the night with all the glittering lights. She had always felt at home in it. Tonight, though, there was something stirring in the darkness. She couldn't explain it, but she felt the need to finish her business for the evening and make it home and lock herself in.

She rose, her knees bearing the marks of the stone floor on them. She had lost track of time as she prayed. Now, though, she realized that she would be late to her appointment if she didn't hurry. She had some business with a lawyer in town and it wouldn't do to get off on the wrong foot.

Pierre de Chauvere was the youngest attorney in a long-standing family business. He had taken over from his father a couple of years earlier and he came highly recommended. As she left the cathedral she made her way to his offices which were housed in an elegant old mansion downtown.

She arrived only a minute or two late and was immediately escorted into his study by his secretary. The room was well-appointed, furnished with luxurious antiques and thick red velvet curtains. She walked over to a large fireplace that was burning cheerily, chasing away the chill of the large room.

"It is a pleasure to make your acquaintance."

Constance turned quickly, unaware that there had been someone else in the room.

A man stood just a few feet from her. He had light colored hair and piercing blue eyes that seemed to look right through her. He was strikingly handsome and his suit was tailored. He bowed. "I am Pierre de Chauvere, at your service."

"I am Constance."

"I'm happy to continue the relationship our ancestors have had," he said.

She looked at him questioningly.

"Both my father and my grandfather did work for your grandparents."

"Oh, I was unaware," she said.

He continued to smile at her.

There was something about him that was dangerous. He was a man to be reckoned with, one that had been touched by darkness. All this she felt intuitively and yet she also sensed that she had nothing to fear from him.

He turned and escorted her to a seat in front of a massive, gold claw-footed desk. He settled himself behind it and then leaned forward, eyes never leaving her face.

"How can I be of service?" he asked.

"I needed a legal advisor. I'm leaving for America soon, and I don't know how long I shall be gone."

"The war?" he asked shrewdly.

She nodded, a sudden lump in her throat. She was going to miss everything about Prague while she was gone – it's mystery, it's magic, all of it. Everything in America was just so new, so steeped in modern technology instead of ancient mysticism. She was sure she wasn't going to like it. She also felt something of the coward for abandoning her country in its darkest hour.

Her father said it was because she was young and sentimental and she hadn't yet learned that age and practicality were more important. She prayed that she never would.

"What things do you need handled?"

"I inherited a piece of property from one of my grandparents. It's in France."

"And you're wondering what you can do to safeguard your title in these coming days?"

She nodded.

"Very little, I'm afraid. In a couple of years it might not even be in France anymore. It might be part of Germany."

She knew that many feared as such.

She lifted her chin defiantly. "We must have faith, trust in God."

"But in addition to trust it's also wise to protect yourself as best you can?"

"Of course, He gave us minds for a reason."

"If you have the documents regarding the property I will see what I can do," he said.

She nodded and pulled a sheaf of papers out of the bag she was carrying with her. She handed them to him, and he took them and put them down on his desk without taking his eyes off her.

"Don't you want to look them over?" she asked.

"No, Constance, I'd prefer to look at you as long as I may."

His forwardness startled her, and she felt her cheeks growing warm.

"I did not mean to embarrass you," he said quickly. "It's just…you are extraordinary, do you know that?"

She could feel a smile spreading across her face, but she didn't answer.

He shook his head as though in a silent self-rebuke. "My apologies. What else might I help you with?"

She took a deep breath. "I have heard rumors of a family heirloom that went missing back sometime during the Renaissance and I want it found."

"What is it?" he asked, frowning slightly.

"A cross necklace dating back to the crusades."

He stared at her for a long minute before finally answering. "Such a thing would be nearly impossible to recover. Even if you had an accurate description the odds of finding a particular cross necklace centuries after it was lost are astronomical."

"Which is why I'm here. I understand that as attorneys go, you are quite the genius at obtaining rare items. Some even call you a miracle worker."

He waved his hand dismissively. "You should not believe such idle gossip."

"Then you won't help me find the necklace?" she asked, working to conceal her disappointment.

"I said it would be nearly impossible. I never said I wouldn't try. I will, however, need more information to go on."

"I can provide that."

"Excellent. Do you have plans for Christmas Eve?"

"No, not with my family already gone. I have to admit, this will be our first Christmas apart."

"Well, why don't you gather together what you have and we can go over it tomorrow night at dinner?"

"Excuse me?"

He smiled. "I, too, have no plans for Christmas Eve and it seems a shame that we should spend it alone. I know I'm being forward, but since you are expecting to leave town soon it wouldn't be prudent to wait until we got to know each other better. I believe time, as they say, is of the essence in this situation."

Her heart had begun to pound in her chest, but she found herself smiling back at him.

"Dinner it is, then," she said.

"Excellent. Six o'clock. I will pick you up."

She nodded and stood. The room which had earlier seemed chilly to her was now very warm. Her mind was swimming with so many thoughts, and she feared that she needed to remove herself from his presence if she hoped to get them under control.

"Until tomorrow then," she said.

"I wait with bated breath," he answered.

She left the office and made her way to the front of the building and outside where she forced herself to take a deep breath of the crisp air. A moment later she turned up the street, already trying to decide what she should wear to the dinner date.

She had gone nearly a block when she paused. Someone was following her. She could feel it. The tiny hairs on the back of her neck had stood on end and a chill raced down her back.

She turned quickly, but there was nothing but shadows behind her, dark and impossible to penetrate with her probing eyes. Was one of them slightly deeper and darker than the others? She wrapped her arms around herself, the cold beginning to move through her.

She was in danger, she could feel it. Something in the darkness wanted to harm her. She gripped her bag tighter, wishing she had a weapon of some sort in it. This was the first time she'd ever felt the need for such a thing, though.

"Who's there?" she asked, her voice coming out as barely more than a whisper.

Only silence answered her though she kept expecting to hear some sound – a mocking laugh, a footfall, anything to prove that she really wasn't alone. She heard nothing, though. After almost a minute had passed she turned and resumed her journey home. Once there she locked windows and doors before falling into a restless sleep.

The next night Constance waited downstairs for Pierre to pick her up. She had chosen a simple but elegant black dress. Unfortunately she didn't have anything to accent it. Her mother had taken all the jewelry with her when she left for America. Constance would very much have liked to adorn the outfit with some pearls.

Pierre arrived right on schedule and she was pleased that he came to the door to greet her instead of sending his chauffer.

"You look radiant," he said with a smile.

Almost immediately she felt herself relaxing. He had a charm about him that was undeniable and when he offered her his arm she gladly took it and let him walk her down the stairs to the waiting car.

Dinner was at one of the most expensive restaurants in Prague. She noticed that Pierre barely touched his food, seemingly much more interested in asking her questions about herself, her family, anything and everything it seemed. When he dropped her back home it seemed far too soon.

The next several weeks passed swiftly in a whirlwind of laughter, music, and dancing. She knew she should be leaving Prague and joining her family in America, but she found it increasingly possible to tear herself away. Her fears about the coming war seemed to fade away as she reveled in Pierre's company. He was incredibly intelligent and educated and she could feel herself falling for him. When she was with him it was as though the entire world fell away and it was just the two of them.

It was a beautiful snowy night that she was sitting in his study while he painted her portrait. She stared at the man who was so intently studying her and she felt warmth deep inside.

He was beautiful and timeless in some odd way she couldn't quite explain. He moved with a grace and a fluidity that she had never seen before in any other. She imagined it would surpass that of even a dancer for the famed Russian ballet.

"I love it when you smile at me like that," he said.

She could feel a blush rising to her cheeks.

"I love that you make me smile like this," she answered.

"I would make you smile that way for all eternity."

She felt the blush deepening and she couldn't stop smiling even if she had wanted to. Pierre was bringing something out in her, thoughts and feelings she had never known before.

When at last he had finished he turned the painting so that she could see it. She was startled to discover that he had painted her as she appeared with one exception. Around her neck she was wearing a beautiful cross necklace.

"I imagined what you would look like wearing the necklace that I will find for you," he said. "Think of it as my promise to you that it shall be found by my hand and that you will wear it in triumph."

"I don't know what to say."

"Say that you like it."

"I love it," she said, daring to meet his eyes.

"I love it, too," he whispered.

For a moment she thought he was going to kiss her. Instead he reached into the pocket of his jacket and pulled out a box. "Until the day that I can give you the cross, I would be honored if you would wear this in its place."

He handed her the box, his fingers brushing hers. She stared at it a moment with so many thoughts and feelings colliding within her.

"Open it," he urged.

She did and gasped when she saw a stunning black pearl pendant inside. The pearl itself was the largest she'd ever seen and when she moved to touch it she felt warmth radiating from it into her fingers.

"It's beautiful," she said.

"Put it on," he urged.

"I couldn't possibly accept so expensive a gift," she murmured in protest.

"Of course you can. After all, it comes from one who cares for you deeply."

He smiled at her and she felt all her resistance melt. Slowly she put on the necklace, savoring the feel of the smooth pearl against the skin of her throat.

"Stunning," he said, his breath catching slightly. He cleared his throat. "I have it under good authority that the pearl has magic to it."

"Really?" she asked, feeling her heart begin to beat a little faster in eager anticipation of what he was going to say next. "What sort of magic?"

"The magic to help you understand your destiny and to make bold decisions in claiming it."

"What do you think destiny has in store for me?" she asked.

"Something wonderful. You are a unique woman with gifts others do not have. You can see what others don't, and you have the courage to do what other's can't."

She felt her breath catch in her throat.

"You are sorely needed here," he continued. "By me, and I would be fool to let you go."

He knelt down on one knee and took her hand in his. "Constance, if you will consent to be my bride I will contact your family immediately and make all the arrangements."

Her head was spinning. Deep down she had known this was where they were heading, but it was all happening so fast. The pearl that had been warm against her skin now felt hot as though it were searing her flesh. She looked down into

Pierre's eyes and she wanted to say "yes", to tell him they'd be together forever.

But whose version of forever?

The strange thought came to her, piercing through the fog that seemed to be enveloping her. Pierre was looking up at her, eyes burning, a look of yearning in them.

"I...I...this is all happening so fast. I need a moment to catch my breath, to think," she finally managed to say.

She could tell he was disappointed, but he nodded and stood. "I understand. It must seem sudden for you, but for me...I've been searching for you for longer than you could know. Of course, you can have some to think about it. I love you and I will await your decision."

"I love you, too," the words burst from her, honest and real. She hadn't meant to say them, but she didn't regret that she had.

He smiled. "Then I have cause to hope that your deliberations will not be lengthy."

She nodded and stepped back. "I need to think. I will see you tomorrow night?"

"Yes."

She turned and left his presence as quickly as she could. She did need air, and to think. Marrying Pierre would almost certainly mean remaining in Prague, and as much as she rejoiced at that idea, she was also frightened by it given that the war was on their doorstep already.

She made her way swiftly to the cathedral, the place where she always went when she needed to pray and focus. The building was empty and she was grateful for the solitude as she approached the altar at the front and when she was just away she slipped to her knees in prayer.

She knew how she felt about Pierre. The decision should have been a simple one, yet there was something that seemed to be fighting her deep down in her soul. Even if she could convince him to leave Europe it would not set aright what she felt in her heart was wrong.

She felt a presence move in the darkness behind her. She stood swiftly. Candles burned brightly at the front of the cathedral and cast a pool of light around her. Ten feet away their influence ended and the darkness swallowed up everything else.

She could feel the thing that was there watching her. She had thought she'd been followed, watched on and off for days, but know she was certain of it.

"Creature of darkness, show yourself. Step into the light," she challenged.

She saw movement and then a moment later a man emerged from the shadows. Only he wasn't a man, he was something else. He was staring intently at her, teeth bared, to expose fangs where his incisors should have been.

She forced herself to stand her ground even though her heart began pounding in fear.

"Calm yourself," he said sharply.

"What are you?"

"I am Raphael. As to what I am, the word you would use is vampire."

"You've been watching me," she accused.

"I have. I must admit that I am curious. How did you sense my presence, the evil within, and yet completely miss it in Pierre?"

For one terrible moment it felt like her heart was going to stop beating forever. Pain knifed through her, real and tangible yet also elusive and ethereal.

"What?" she finally managed to whisper.

"He, too, is a vampire, and yet you have not fled from his presence."

"What you say can't be true."

Yet, she knew with a flash of insight that it was. It explained her hesitation earlier that evening. Something deep down in her soul had known, although she chastised herself for not having known the moment she met him that he was touched by evil. She was usually very quick to perceive such things.

"I cannot be with him," she whispered to herself.

The pearl grew warm and that warmth felt like it was radiating through her. "I must join my family in California," she said.

The pearl warmed her even more.

"That is the safest thing for you to do," Raphael said.

With the decision made an urgency settled upon her. She should have left days ago, but the burgeoning relationship with Pierre had kept her long past the leaving time.

"I must leave in the morning."

She was halfway to the back of the cathedral before Raphael called after her, "Where are you going tonight?"

"To end things," she answered.

She had no idea why Raphael had told her the truth about Pierre. Frankly, it made little sense unless he was trying to hurt the other vampire. There was no reason he'd be looking out for her.

"Safe journey, Lady of Bryas," he called after her.

It took all of her willpower to keep walking and not turn around and ask him how he knew about her land in France. It was possible Pierre had told him, but more likely that he had been spying and found out. Either way it didn't matter. What did matter was talking to Pierre immediately.

Even as she made her way to Pierre's home a part of her urged her to head for the airport and escape as swiftly as she could. She dismissed the frightened clamoring in her mind, though. Pierre wouldn't hurt her. She was sure of that.

The snow had started coming down harder and when she made it to the mansion that served as both his office and his home she was out of breath from having walked so quickly slogging through it.

He answered the door himself, surprise lighting up his features. "I had not expected to see you again tonight."

"May I come in?" she asked, feeling suddenly self-conscious.

"Of course," he said, brow furrowing as he stepped back to allow her entrance. He followed her to the study. Once there she turned, forcing herself to face him.

"What's wrong?" he asked.

"Is it true that you are a vampire?" There was no use mincing words. The man had asked her to marry him, and they had several things they needed to discuss honestly.

Several moments passed as he stared at her. She waited, expecting him to deny it. Instead he slowly nodded.

"I am. And I would very much like to know who told you."

"That's not important. What's important is that you should have told me."

"Had you consented to marry me, I would have. It's not a secret that is shared lightly."

"You kill people? Feed on their blood?"

He sighed. "No. Fortunately there are much more civilized options available to us. I get my sustenance from a local hospital which supplies me with blood that was donated."

"But you are undead?" she questioned.

"Why don't we sit down?" he asked, sounding old and tired in that moment. "Clearly whoever you talked to didn't actually explain this condition to you."

She sat, prepared to hear him out. He spoke for nearly half an hour and when he was finished she understood.

But it didn't change anything.

Pierre looked at her, eyes pleading, when he finally stopped talking. "Can you still love me?" he asked.

"I do love you, Pierre," she said softly. "I can't marry you, though. I would wish that instead we could remain friends."

Something dark and ugly flashed across his face for just a moment, and she forced herself not to react. Perhaps she had been wrong about him not hurting her. After all, she hadn't managed to sense the evil in him until someone else pointed it out.

"We can be good, dear friends. I, of course, will remain your attorney and will continue to search for your family's necklace. I hope you understand, though, that I will not give up the hope of something more."

She knew there was no hope for him there. Being his wife was not part of her destiny, she could feel that with complete certainty. There was, however, going to be no convincing him of that. He would continue to pursue. Which was yet another reason why she should be headed to California by morning.

She reached up to the pearl necklace. "I should give this back to you," she said as her fingers fumbled with the clasp.

He shook his head. "No, it is my gift to you, and my promise. You will wear it."

"Thank you."

His telephone rang and with a frown he moved to answer it. The conversation was swift, lasting ten seconds only, but when he hung up Constance instinctively knew that something had changed.

"What's wrong?" she asked, rising from the couch where she had been sitting.

"German soldiers are invading. They will be in the city tomorrow."

And just like that the reality of the world around them that she'd been blissfully ignoring for the past few weeks came crashing down around them. Fear pulsed through her.

"I need to go home and grab a couple of things before I leave," she said.

"It might be too late to leave," he answered grimly. "You should stay here. I will protect you."

"No, my family is expecting me. I need to go to them."

"You cannot make it out on foot, not in this storm," he said. "Dawn is coming and I will be forced to sleep. I don't have time to get you out. I can give you my car, though."

He reached into his desk for a set of keys and then quickly crossed and handed them to her.

"I can't," she protested.

"You must. I love you and I will see you safe. When you make it out, call me. And call again when you get to California."

"I will," she promised.

His face contorted into a look of pain. "If you are going, then you must leave now."

Her heart was pounding. There was so much happening, changing. This moment in time would never come again. She leaned forward and kissed Pierre, brushing her lips softly against his. When she pulled away he was staring at her in bewilderment.

"Be safe," she told him breathlessly.

He nodded and she turned and left.

She'd only driven a car a handful of times, but there was almost noone on the streets and she made it home within ten minutes. She raced inside, grabbed the few things she absolutely needed, including her passport and what money she had left, and made it back to the car.

She realized she had no idea what direction the German soldiers would be coming from. She prayed as she began her drive out of town that God would lead her where she needed to go.

The snow was still falling fast and her tires spun from time-to-time. When she finally put the city behind her she began to breathe a sigh of relief until she noticed lights up ahead of her.

Heart in her throat she pulled up to a couple of vehicles blocking the road. Three men were clustered off to the side while a fourth approached her with flashlight in hand.

"Where are you going, Miss?" he asked in a heavy German accent.

"To see my grandmother in the country. We just had word that she is dying and I need to be there."

"I'm sorry. We cannot let anyone through," he said.

She felt her heart sinking. There was no way she could ram the cars aside and make it. She needed them to let her go.

"Please, I have to be there," she said, forcing a few tears out. Deep inside a feeling of dread was building. She had the overwhelming belief that if she didn't make it out now that she was going to be one of the first casualties of the German invasion.

His eyes drifted from her face and she realized he was staring at her pearl necklace.

"I can't," he repeated.

She touched the necklace. "I will give you this if you let me go," she said.

He quickly glanced over at his comrades then back at her. "Okay," he said, nodding.

"Move the car!" he called over to the other men.

One got in and backed one of the cars up slightly, forming a gap large enough for her to drive through. She took off the necklace and regretfully handed it to the soldier. Pierre would understand.

She drove past the roadblock without a backward glance. Behind her the home she loved stood on the brink of being changed forever, and the man that she loved would be in danger as well. All she could do, though, was go forward. She would make it, escape to California to be with her family who'd had the good sense to leave earlier.

Real tears began to stream down her face as she wondered if she'd ever see Prague or Pierre again.

"I'm sorry, I'm so sorry," she whispered as she saw the first rays of the sun break the horizon.

The Christmas of Candy Jewelry

California, The Day After Thanksgiving

Becca Sinclair was sitting in her supervisor's office at The Zone theme park wondering exactly what she'd done to end up there. She kicked her legs back and forth, unable to contain the restless energy that was pulsing through her. It was the day after Thanksgiving, or, as everyone liked to say, the beginning of the Christmas Zone. It was getting hard to contain her excitement.

Her sister, Bunni, who worked for the Escape Channel! was going to be visiting for a few days in between filming specials. Her friends Candace and Josh were going to both be coming home from college for the Christmas break, and things were going really well with her boyfriend, Roger. So well, in fact, that she was struggling to figure out exactly what to give him for Christmas.

The door opened and Martha, an older woman who was one of the cart and counter service supervisors, came in and sat down. She leaned across the desk.

"Becca, what are we going to do with you?" she asked, sounding tired.

"Ummm...put me in charge of the Muffin Mansion?"

Martha actually smiled. "Maybe one of these days, but I'm more worried about today."

"I don't know why I'm here," Becca said.

"You're here because we need to have a serious talk about a new item that is being installed in the Game Zone as we speak."

Given that the Muffin Mansion was in a different part of the park, Becca wasn't sure what something in the Game Zone could have to do with her. "Is it a Muffin Mansion kiosk?" she asked.

"No, but that's not a bad idea. They're installing a new game machine. You know those kind where you have to manipulate the claw so that it drops and picks up a stuffed animal?"

"Yeah."

"Well, it's going to be one of those games, only it won't be filled with stuffed animals."

"What will it be filled with?" Becca asked.

"Jewelry, a few pieces of fancy costume jewelry purchased from some antique stores to tantalize, but most of it will actually be candy jewelry."

Becca felt her eyes grow wide. "Like the ring pops and candy bracelets?"

"Exactly."

"I love the ring pops," Becca said a little breathlessly.

"You love all things sugar, which is why we're having this little conversation," Martha said sternly.

Becca felt herself deflate and she slid down in her chair a bit. "You want me to stay away from it."

"Yes. I know it presents a big temptation. It's the only sugar in the park whose distribution is not controlled or monitored by referees."

"I can't promised anything," Becca grumbled.

Martha narrowed her eyes at her. "Every few months it seems that somehow, despite all our efforts, you get hold of some sugar and you go completely crazy, tearing the place up."

It sounded harsh, but it was fair. Sugar made Becca hyper, crazy hyper. She was allergic to it and even the smallest amount sent her into overdrive and she couldn't always be held responsible for her actions afterward. Everyone at The Zone went out of their way to make sure she couldn't get hold of any. Now she was finding out there was a whole machine of candy and the only things that stood between her and it were some quarters and a metal claw. She could feel herself start to twitch just thinking about it.

"Becca, I really don't want to have to post a security guard there just because of you," Martha said.

"I promise I'll be on my best behavior," Becca said, a little angry and a little sad at the same time.

"That's a good girl. Okay, you can go back to work now."

Becca forced herself to her feet, trying to put the thought of the sugary temptation out of her mind. It was a lot harder to do than even those who knew her well would guess.

When she made it back into the Muffin Mansion all the other referees stopped and stared at her. Finally Gib who always managed to look and sound something like a pirate spoke up.

"And how are ye holdin' up?" he asked.

"Fine," she said, putting on a perky smile.

He glanced at some of the others then turned back to her. "Did they tell you about..."

"Yes, I know about the candy jewelry machine."

"Oh, good. And everything is..."

"Good," she told him.

"Good." He turned and glanced at the others. "See 'tis no problem."

She could tell from their wide-eyed expressions that none of the others believed it.

Roger wasn't working that day or she was sure he would have stuck up for her, even if he privately harbored doubts. Just thinking about him made her smile. She thought about him the rest of the afternoon and when her shift was over and he walked through the door it was like she had magically summoned him.

She squealed with joy and ran into his arms. He picked her up and spun her around, something he couldn't have once done without tripping or dropping her. Roger had once been famous for being the biggest klutz in The Zone. Their friend Candace had helped him gain confidence and eventually get over that. Now Becca and Roger were taking a ballroom dance class together and he was actually the better dancer.

She waved goodbye to Gib and the others as she went out the door with Roger. She started to head Off field to the Locker Rooms so she could change clothes and grab her stuff, but Roger instead steered her toward the front of the park.

"Where are we going?" she asked.

"Don't you at least want to see it?"

"How do you know about the new candy machine? You weren't working today."

"Gib called to warn me."

She shouldn't have been surprised. Arm-in-arm they strolled into The Game Zone section of the park and as they neared the candy game she saw the other referees growing agitated as they saw them.

At last they were standing in front of the big yellow box that had so many sparkly things inside. Her eyes, though, were on the mounds of candy jewelry.

"Oh," she said, a little sigh escaping her as she stared at the candy rings especially and imagined the taste of them.

"It's a quarter a play. I've got exactly one quarter in my pocket if you want it," Roger said.

"I shouldn't," she said as she held out her hand.

He put the quarter in it and she quickly put it in the machine. She grabbed the controls and manipulated the claw until it was directly over a lovely cherry red candy ring. She was practically salivating as she dropped the claw.

She watched, her heart pounding, eyes glued to the action inside the machine. The claw plunged into the mound of candy sending a little shiver down her spine. Then ever so slowly it raised up. It cleared the mound of candy and she blinked in dismay.

"No!" she said, fighting the urge to hit the control panel.

Instead of her beautiful, shiny red candy ring a small jewelry box was lodged in the claw. It dropped it in the shoot and a moment later she pulled it out of the bin at the bottom.

She stared at the small box and tried to hold back a couple of tears of frustration.

"Open it and at least see what you got," Roger said quietly.

She opened the lid. Inside was a giant black pearl on a necklace. It was beautiful and actually looked a lot more real than some of the other jewelry displayed inside the cage.

"If it was real, I'd give it to my sister. She loves pearls," Becca said.

"Why don't you take it as your white elephant gift to the Christmas party?"

"That's a good idea," she said.

She touched the pearl. It was warm against her fingers.

I'm going to get all the candy in there, she thought to herself, as she pictured covering her fingers with ring pops.

"Becca, you okay?"

She closed the jewelry box and looked at Roger. "Fine, why?"

"You just seemed to space out there for a minute and I was worried."

"Sorry."

"It's okay. Let's go grab your stuff and I'll take you to dinner."

"Okay, but then I have to get home. Unfortunately I have a morning shift tomorrow so I've got to be here by six."

Becca tossed and turned all night and when the alarm went off in the morning she awoke from a dream that the candy jewelry dispenser had malfunctioned and was showering her with all the candy. Sometimes it could be really frustrating that the thing she loved was the thing that she was allergic to.

Even though she was supposed to stay away from the machine she found herself emptying all the change except the quarters out of her purse. She added the other coins to her bank that sat on top of her dresser.

She arrived at work twenty minutes early. She had time to kill. She stared at the quarters in her purse and finally put them in her pocket even as she told herself she was just going to look at the candy machine.

It was still dark outside as she walked through the park. There were only a handful of safety lights on. By one of the carnival rides in the Game Zone were some maintenance tools and a ladder. There was no sign of the worker, though, which was good. At last Becca was standing in front of the machine and she could actually feel herself starting to salivate as she imagined the taste of all the different candies inside.

Maybe just one, she thought to herself as her fingers slipped the quarter into the slot. She maneuvered the claw into place before dropping it into the pile of candy. It rose a second later and it was completely empty.

"No!" she said, and this time she did ball up her fist and lightly pound on the machine.

She was already ready with her second quarter. It and the third one came up empty as well.

Her final quarter went into the slot and she gritted her teeth as she tried to maneuver the claw, nudging it slightly this way and that before it finally went plummeting.

It rose with three of the ring pops wedged inside. She could feel her spirits soaring.

And then the claw jerked to a halt. Instead of traveling over to the shoot and dropping her candy in it the claw just hovered above the pile of candy, frozen. She tried the controls, but nothing worked. Finally she shook it slightly, but that didn't do anything either.

"They're mine, I won them!" she yelled at the machine.

She needed to get help, a maintenance guy or something. Of course, if she did get someone to come help there was no way they'd give her the candy she'd won.

And she had paid for that candy and won it fair and square.

She thought of the ladder and the tools she had seen and she ran to get them. When she came back she set up the ladder and climbed to the top of the machine. There she was able to use a screwdriver to take off the lid which she carefully set down on the ground. Then she climbed back up the ladder and leaned over into the machine, trying to reach the claw with her candy. It was just out of reach and she couldn't reach the mound below it, either. She climbed to the very top rung and leaned farther.

Her fingers brushed against the claw mechanism and suddenly it whirred to life, opening its jaws and releasing her candy back into the pile before returning to its starting position.

"No!"

She reached for her fallen candy and a moment later began to flail as she realized she was off balance.

She landed head first on the candy pile. After a moment she was able to flip herself around. The ladder fell, clattering to the ground. It was okay, she could still climb out and over and drop to the ground. The machine was only about eight feet tall. It would be okay.

She glanced down and saw a red ruby ring pop. *Her* red ruby ring pop. Her fist closed around it and a moment later she had torn open the plastic, put the ring on her finger, and was licking away at it.

With her free hand she was tearing into one of the other packages a moment later. She put the second ring pop on another finger and now she had two she could lick while she worked on getting ring pops for the rest of the fingers.

She became so engrossed that she didn't notice what was happening around her until she had rings on all ten fingers. That was when she heard somebody cough.

Martha, Gib, and several of her other coworkers were standing around the machine that she was wedged inside.

Before she could pull one of the pops out of her mouth to say something, anything, Gib turned to the others. "Alright, the official time is three minutes to six. Who was it that had down that she'd be *inside* the machine before six a.m.?"

"That would be me," Martha said.

At that point everyone reached into a pocket, pulled out a five dollar bill, and handed it over to her. She pocketed the money with a mildly amused grin and just shook her head at Becca.

Just then a maintenance guy came scurrying up. "Hey, what's going on here? Who took my equipment? What are you all staring-"

He stopped midsentence as he spied Becca inside of the machine.

Gib put a hand on his shoulder. "Didn't I tell you to watch out for Becca?"

A Christmas Psalm

California, The Second Friday of December

Traci Walters loved Fridays. Being a detective's wife was a tough job and her husband's schedule was wildly unpredictable. He often ended up stuck working over the weekends. Every week, though, he did everything he could to be home on time on Friday so they were guaranteed Friday evening to themselves. It was the one time she could count on spending time with him so it was precious to her. Over the years he'd only had to miss a handful of their date nights.

Tonight should be interesting. Her sister and brother-in-law were babysitting the twins and she and Mark were scheduled to go to a Christmas play at Cindy's church. Traci had never been to a Christmas play before, and when Cindy had mentioned it at lunch a week before Traci had jumped at the chance to go.

Mark came through the door right on schedule and whistled when he saw her in her new red dress. She did a slow spin and he gave her an admiring grin.

"This is worth coming home for, even if I have to go to a church play," he said.

She kissed him. "It could be fun."

He looked skeptical, and she didn't blame him. Neither of them had been raised in religious households or had friends who were religious. That had changed, though. Cindy and Jeremiah had become two of their closest friends and religion was a big part of both of their lives.

Traci had been growing more and more curious about God and the whole church thing the last year or so. Cindy was often maddeningly slow to give her more information, though. She knew the other woman wasn't trying to be preachy, which she really, really appreciated, but sometimes Traci wanted more information than Cindy was giving her. Maybe she could get some of her questions answered tonight.

Twenty minutes later they were walking inside the church. Now that she was there Traci felt a little hesitant as she looked at all the unfamiliar faces. Around her people were greeting each other and she definitely felt a bit out of place and intimidated.

She was about to turn to Mark and admit that maybe coming had been a mistake when she heard someone call her name. She turned and saw Cindy wave at her. She was standing next to the door, passing out programs to people who went inside the sanctuary.

Relieved to see a familiar face Traci headed her way, pulling Mark along with her.

She hugged Cindy when they reached her.

"I'm so glad you could come," Cindy said.

"Thanks for telling me about it," Traci said.

"Jeremiah is saving seats for all of us down at the front," Cindy said as she gave them both programs. "I'll be there once everything starts."

Traci took a deep breath and smiled at her. "This is going to be great," she said.

Cindy nodded vigorously. "Wait until you see what the drama department has pulled off this year. Gus and the others have really outdone themselves."

Traci could feel her excitement levels building again. A line was beginning to form behind them so she gave Cindy another smile and then pulled Mark inside. She scanned the pews that were closer to the stage, looking for Jeremiah. As she moved to her left to head down the one aisle, Mark suddenly stopped.

"What is it?" she asked, turning to him.

"Right here is where it all happened," he said, pointing to the floor.

She glanced down. "Where what all happened?"

"Where Cindy tripped over that dead body, screamed, Jeremiah came running, called 911, and Paul and I were sent out to investigate."

She sucked in her breath. "This is where it all started," she said.

"Yes."

None of our lives have ever been the same, she thought to herself. She wondered briefly what would have happened if that man had been murdered somewhere else so that Cindy never tripped over him and Jeremiah never came to her rescue.

Her mind started spinning as she thought about all the possibilities. Paul and Mark would never have met Cindy and Jeremiah. Which meant that nearly a year later they wouldn't have uncovered the plot revolving around the Green Pastures Camp and Paul wouldn't have raced up there and gotten himself killed.

Paul would still be alive, and Mark wouldn't know that his partner wasn't who he said he was.

Sudden tears came to her eyes, and she inhaled sharply.

If things hadn't happened that way, though, who knew what else might have gone wrong. Without Jeremiah and Mark worrying about her, Cindy might have been killed by her kidnappers when she went to Hawaii on vacation. For that matter Traci might have been killed, too, by the police officer who had kidnapped her if Mark had been the one to take the call about the dead guy at Joseph's house during his big charity kick-off before the whole Green Pastures thing happened.

"Traci, what's wrong?" Mark asked.

She realized that she was standing, rooted to the spot. "All our lives were forever altered that day," she said.

"I hadn't really thought about it, but I guess they were."

"It's just, a lot to take in," she said.

"I understand. We can discuss it if you like, but let's stop blocking traffic and go find Jeremiah."

She nodded, head still spinning.

As it turned out Jeremiah had saved them all seats in the second row. It was close enough to have a great view and yet not as exposed as the front row.

Mark sat down next to Jeremiah while Traci left a place for Cindy to sit next to her. Normally she would encourage Cindy to sit next to Jeremiah, but she wanted to be able to ask her questions during the play if she needed to.

She opened her program and tried to read, but her mind was still racing and she couldn't focus on the words in front of her.

"It should be starting any moment now," Mark said a couple of minutes later.

There was a sudden commotion behind them. A woman's anxious voice said, "Where's John?"

There was some more voices, raised in agitation and as she, Mark and Jeremiah turned to look she heard an anguished cry, "Someone has taken my baby!"

Mark was out of his seat in a flash and Jeremiah was right behind him.

Traci felt her heart racing and she could feel the other woman's panic. Her mind flashed to her two babies and she had to take a deep breath, reminding herself that they were safe.

She stood up and joined Mark and Jeremiah. If they worked fast, maybe they could find the baby before it had been harmed.

Cindy came running down the aisle, her face ashen. Everyone was standing up, talking all at once. After a minute Cindy turned to her. "They have another child who's in the play, Amelia. She's five."

"Let's go find her," Traci said. "Maybe she knows what happened. Even if she doesn't, her parents are going to want to see that she's safe."

"Okay."

Traci turned and followed Cindy.

"She should be in the choir room with the others, getting ready," Cindy said.

Seconds later they burst into the choir room. A man who looked to be the director had been talking to a group of men, women, and children. He stopped when they entered. "What's wrong?" he asked.

"Is Amelia here?" Cindy asked.

"Yes."

"We need her to come with us," Cindy said.

"Amelia, can you come here?" the man called.

A little girl dressed like an angel walked over. "What is it?" she asked.

"Your mother needs to see you," Cindy said, putting a hand on the girl's shoulder.

Together they walked the little girl into the sanctuary and up to her parents who were now tightly surrounded by people.

"What's going on?" Amelia asked, eyes wide and frightened.

Mark turned to her and got down on one knee. "Amelia, honey. Someone took your brother from his car seat here in the pew. Did you see who?"

Amelia frowned at him. "I took him out of his car seat."

Suddenly all noise ceased and all eyes focused on the little girl. "When did you do that?" Mark asked her.

"Right before I went back to the choir room. I told Mom we needed a baby Jesus because the other baby was sick and couldn't come."

Amelia's mother was staring at her. "I remember you saying something about the other baby being sick," she said, her voice shaking.

Amelia nodded. "Then I took John and I put him backstage in the manger so he could play baby Jesus."

Cindy spun and ran and Traci followed. They went through the door next to the stage, made a couple of quick turns and then saw all the props for the play, including a manger. They ran up to it and inside they saw a peacefully sleeping baby.

Traci reached down and picked him up. "There's a lot of fuss tonight, and it seems it's all about you," she said, hearing her own voice shake.

Together they quickly made their way back into the sanctuary. Amelia's mother cried as Traci handed her the child.

Slowly everyone calmed down and returned to their seats amidst tears and laughter.

"That's one mystery I'm glad is solved," Mark muttered as they sat back down in their pew.

Before the play could start the mother came and crouched down next to Traci. "Thank you. I'm told that it was you who thought to go get Amelia."

"I knew you'd want her close," Traci said.

The woman handed her a necklace with a large, black pearl on it. "Please, take this as a thank you. It's not much."

"I can't take a pearl necklace," Traci protested.

"I'm pretty sure it's not real. I got it in a white elephant gift exchange at a party I went to the other day. It's just, I need to give you something."

"Thank you," Traci said, taking the necklace from her.

The woman nodded, stood and disappeared back into her pew.

Traci touched the pearl which grew warm in a moment. Warmth flooded through her as well. She put the necklace on. A moment later Cindy joined them.

"I'm sorry for all the stress," Cindy said. "Not exactly what I would have wanted for your first visit to my church."

"It's fine," Traci said with a smile. "It's weird, but I'm just getting the strangest feeling that I belong here."

Cindy's smile was dazzling. "That's great. Well, I hope you like the play. It's about to start. I love your necklace, by the way."

"Thank you," Traci said with a smile. "For everything."

The Twenty-Third of Christmas

California, December 23rd

Geanie Coulter loved holidays. She always had. She was a firm believer in celebrating whatever you could whenever you could. When she was bored she'd even make up little holidays for herself and dress up for them. Of course, she usually didn't tell anyone what she was doing. On last Dress Like a Vampire Thursday she had worn a black velvet miniskirt, a blood red satin blouse, and red fishnet stockings. She had put on a white cream makeup base from one of her Halloween makeup kits and had painted her lips blood red. Everyone had told her she looked pretty, a few might have muttered something less polite under their breaths, but no one had guessed she was dressing that way for a particular purpose. Well, no one except for her husband, Joseph.

He had taken one look at her ensemble and said "I vant to suck your blood," in his best Bela Lugosi impersonation.

She loved that he got it. In many ways she felt like he was the first person who had ever really gotten her in general. She had friends, some good ones, but she knew most of them viewed her as a bit of an oddity. That was fine. She'd grown up used to that. It was nice, though, to finally have someone who didn't. Joseph celebrated her eccentricities, her need to amuse herself. In September he had even surprised her and picked her up for lunch dressed as a pirate on International Talk Like a Pirate Day. She had been so happy that he was participating in her mania that she'd teared up and had to excuse herself to the bathroom for a minute because no one wanted to see a pirate cry.

Joseph was wonderful and the last several months since they were married had been amazing. Which made his behavior the last couple of days that much stranger.

"Earth to Geanie?"

She blinked and looked over at Cindy. "I'm sorry, what did you say?"

"I asked how things were going with the bulletin."

"Oh, fine," Geanie said, glancing back at her computer screen. She was working on finishing up the Sunday bulletin which had to be done today because she was off the next day.

"If you need help with the copying machine or the folding machine just let me know."

Geanie glanced back at Cindy. "You're probably busier than I am today."

Cindy just shrugged but Geanie knew that it was true. Cindy was the church secretary, a job that came with so much stress that they couldn't pay Geanie to do that job.

"So, your family is flying in tomorrow morning?" Cindy asked.

"Yes. Joseph doesn't have family so he's flying mine out here to spend Christmas with us."

"What's wrong?" Cindy asked quietly. "You don't sound very excited and you haven't seemed...yourself...the last couple of days."

"Is it that obvious?"

"Yeah."

Geanie sighed. "Joseph's been acting strange and it's starting to worry me."

Before Cindy could say anything in response the door to the office flew open, slamming hard as it bounced against the wall.

Geanie jumped, noticing that Cindy did, too. The youth pastor, Dave, walked in and headed straight for the copier with a bunch of papers clutched in his fist. He didn't greet either of them or even glance their way which was unusual.

"Dave, you okay?" Cindy called out.

"Fine," he said in a voice that sounded anything but.

Geanie shrugged as Cindy glanced over at her. Geanie had no idea whether they should just stay out of his way or if they should actually try more aggressively to talk to him.

From the look on her face Cindy was just as much at a loss as she was. Slowly Geanie stood up and walked over to Dave.

"What's wrong?" she asked when she was standing right behind him.

He jumped and twisted around to face her. "Don't startle me like that," he growled.

"Okay, whatever this is, you need to take a deep breath before you snap at one of the parishioners. You're lucky we're coworkers," Geanie said.

"I'm sorry," Dave mumbled.

"Okay, but what's wrong?"

"I can't talk about it," he said.

"Can't or won't?" she questioned.

He took a deep breath. "Won't," he said, refusing to meet her eyes.

Geanie felt her frustration growing. She had two evasive men in her life currently and that was two too many.

"When you are ready to talk, we're here," she said, forcing herself to let it go.

"Thanks," he said.

She turned and walked back to her desk.

That night after Geanie and Joseph had cleaned up dinner they walked into the living room where Geanie sat down on the couch, eyeing Joseph. He hadn't been able to sit still all through dinner. He'd been fidgeting nonstop which wasn't like him. Now he wasn't sitting down on the couch next to her, but was standing, a look of anticipation on his face.

"You've been acting weird lately. It's freaking me out. What's going on with you?" Geanie asked. She needed some answers from him.

"Sorry to freak you out. I've just been very busy. I'll make it up to you. I know! Do you want to play a game?" he asked, a touch of excitement in his voice at the last.

She stared at him, wondering what was going on in his head. She loved games; he knew that. Was he genuinely wanting to play or was this just to distract her so she'd stop asking questions?

"What did you have in mind?" she asked.

"I'll show you," he said. He moved over to a cabinet where they kept the board games, opened it, and pulled out Clue. He brought it over and put it down on the coffee table in front of her.

He sat down on the couch next to her then opened the box and pulled out the board and all the pieces. The cards he left in the box and she started to reach for them when he stopped her.

"No, we've already got the cards that we need," he said picking up the envelope that was used to hold the guilty cards. He put it down in the middle of the board.

"Joseph, what are you talking about?" she asked him.

He put the lid back on the box and moved it to an end table. On the board he swiftly put everything into place with exception of the game piece for Miss Scarlet which he moved into the library.

"That should start you off right," he said.

73

"Joseph, what is going on?" she demanded.

He gave her a huge grin. "I know that you enjoy mysteries, but you're never the one who gets to solve them," he said. "That changes now."

"What do you mean?"

"You get to solve the mystery that will help you find your Christmas present. Each room on this board corresponds to a room in this house that holds a clue that you need."

"You're kidding, right?"

"No. And I must say it has been fiendishly hard to plan this and keep you in the dark," he said.

She leaned forward and kissed him.

"What was that for? You don't even know what you're getting yet."

"For being you. I'm sorry I ever worried that you were being, well, *not* you."

He smiled at her. "It's our first Christmas as a married couple. Did you really think I could just do something ordinary to celebrate?"

She should never have doubted him for a second. She jumped to her feet, excitement rushing through her. "I'm off to the library," she said.

Joseph smiled as he stood up. He would only have a moment to plant his final clue in the kitchen. He hadn't wanted to risk her finding it earlier. He pulled the black pearl pendant out of his pocket. He had seen Traci wearing it at the

Christmas play at the church. He'd bought it from her because it made the perfect last prop for his whole staged clue hunt.

He was going to have to give Traci some more money, though. He'd convinced her to part with it for fifty dollars. He could have ordered one, but he hadn't wanted to risk packages coming to the house. He was pretty sure once he'd examined it more closely, though, that what Traci had thought was costume jewelry was actually the real deal.

The moment he had touched it he had felt a warm glow and he had seen exactly how much fun he and Geanie were going to have on their anniversary trip to Tahiti. That was his Christmas present to her. And even as he hid the pearl in the kitchen he could feel that this was going to be a very special trip for them both.

A Christmas Witch

Italy, One Year From Now

Samantha Ryan had lived through a crazy year. When her adoptive parents had suggested that they all could use a change of scenery and that spending Christmas abroad might be fun, she had jumped at the chance. Her mother had a distant cousin who had a villa just outside Urbania and he had offered its use. It was a beautiful home and the caretaker had been most gracious to her upon her arrival.

Unfortunately everyone else was still stuck in Boston where they'd been snowed in. She had been helping to consult on a case for the F.B.I. in Los Angeles, and had flown out from there. A dark magic user had actually stolen a real magic object, an antique pearl pendant that was exceptionally old and able to show one their destiny. What Samantha had seen the first time she'd touched the pearl had been nothing short of wonderful which was good.

She had the pearl necklace with her. They didn't know who the witch had stolen it from, but it was far too powerful to just be let loose in the world even if they did know who had previously owned it. Samantha would have to figure out what to do with it once the holiday was over and they were all back home.

If the weather forecast held true everyone else should be able to fly out in two days, making it just in time for Christmas. In the meantime she was taking advantage of the alone time to do some last minute Christmas shopping and to explore the town.

With a population under 10,000 Urbania wasn't large, but the hustle and bustle of Christmastime made it seem vibrant and teeming with people. After having lunch at a charming little restaurant she found herself at a market watching an old fashioned puppet show. Although she didn't normally enjoy puppets there was a quaint charm to this particular show and she found herself laughing along. She didn't understand the language, but she didn't have to thanks to the precision with which the puppeteer managed to portray action and the emotions of the characters.

At last the play came to an end and regretfully she turned to go, wondering what other surprises might be in store for her. She was thinking about getting a pastry from one of the vendors selling them.

Suddenly she felt a ripple go through the air around her. It was like a wave on the ocean the way it moved. Somewhere nearby was another magic user. She turned, scanning the crowd. Whoever it was would have sensed her as well.

The hair on the back of her neck lifted and she twisted around to see an old woman dressed in black staring at her.

Samantha started to raise her hands defensively, but the old woman's manner did not strike her as threatening, and she slowly lowered them.

"You are a good person," the old woman said, making it sound more like a statement than a question.

"I try to be," Samantha answered, wondering what the woman's game was.

"You help people for a living, save them."

"Yes, I'm a police officer, a detective," Samantha said.

The old woman had a lot of power. She had so much of it that Samantha would never have thought to find someone like her in a tiny place like this.

"You will help me and my granddaughter. Come, come, you will see."

"I don't think I'm who you're looking for," Samantha said, suspicious of the woman and her motives.

"But you must help, of course you'll help."

"And why do you think so?" Samantha asked.

"Because you are a good Christian witch," the old lady said earnestly. "You will help Befana."

"I'm a Christian, but I'm not a witch," Samantha protested.

"Of course you are. I feel your power."

"I might be a magic user, but I'm not a witch," Samantha said, trying to stay calm.

"Befana needs you, please come with me, and I will explain," the old woman said, clearly getting more distressed.

Samantha was used to being wary around other magic users, but there was something about the old woman that seemed so sincere. She took a deep breath. It was unlikely that she could pose a real threat to Samantha. Her granddaughter might be a different story, but Samantha decided to risk it.

She nodded and the old woman smiled at her, took her arm, and began to lead her through the crowds.

As they passed by one shop Samantha noticed something odd. In the window instead of displaying a Christmas tree or lights there was a display of hag witches, many on brooms. There looked to be dolls and puppets and ceramic figures. Two more shops that they passed had similar things in their windows surrounded by the normal Christmas decorations. She wondered why she hadn't noticed the witch figures earlier.

Probably because I wasn't thinking about witches, she realized. Her mom had told her that the town had some "interesting" holiday traditions. She wondered if this could be part of them.

They walked a little while more and then turned down a side street. They finally arrived outside a modest looking house and the old woman opened the door. Samantha could feel a wave of energy. There was another magic user in the house.

"Come in, come in," the old woman said eagerly.

Just inside the entrance there were half a dozen brooms of varying sizes and shapes lined up neatly against the wall. There was a narrow staircase leading to the next floor and the steps creaked as a young woman who was probably three or four years younger than Samantha came down them, speaking in Italian.

When she reached the bottom her eyes grew wide and she stared at Samantha for a moment before turning to the old woman.

"Grandmother, who is this?"

"You no listen to me, so I find a witch your age. You will listen to her maybe."

Samantha opened her mouth to say that she was not a witch, but before she could say anything the girl burst into tears and ran past them and out the door.

The old woman threw her hands into the air and a torrent of Italian came out of her."

Samantha had no idea what was going on, but she decided she was probably going to get answers faster from the granddaughter.

"I'll go talk to her," she said, laying her hand on the old woman's shoulder.

"Yes, yes. You will talk some sense into her," the old woman said.

Samantha walked outside. She glanced up and down, but there was no sign of the granddaughter. She held out her hand and felt the swirling energies that the young woman had left in her wake. It would be easy to track her through them.

Ten minutes later Samantha found her sitting on the edge of an ancient looking water fountain. She looked up and saw Samantha coming and quickly wiped away her tears.

"I'm not sure what's going on here, but I'd like to help," Samantha said. "So, let's start over. I'm Samantha."

"Sofia."

Samantha frowned. "You're Grandmother kept saying I had to help Befana, I was under the impression that was your name."

"No, but that's who she wants me to be."

"I don't understand. I'm just here on vacation and I frankly had no idea what she was talking about."

"You don't know the story of La Befana?" Sofia asked.

"I'm afraid not. Would you tell me?"

Sofia nodded, and took a quavering breath, tears threatening to spill down her cheeks again.

Samantha touched her arm and sent waves of warm, calming energy over the other woman. Sofia gaped at her in surprise, but her posture relaxed considerably.

"I've never met another witch besides my grandmother," Sofia said.

"I tried to tell your grandmother, I'm not a witch, just a magic user. I'm actually a Christian."

Sofia frowned. "So are grandmother and I. Why do you say that as though you cannot be both a Christian and a witch?"

Samantha took a deep breath. This was obviously a cultural difference, possibly even a difference in the meanings of the word witch. "Where I come from people who think of themselves as witches would not also think of themselves as Christians. A few wiccans and pagans might use the word witch to describe themselves although they would be mistaken in doing so. A witch is a magic user who uses the power for their own gain. Most people I think of as witches are drawn to the dark and there's nothing religious about what they do."

Sofia shook her head. "That is very different."

"Why don't you tell me the story of Befana?" Samantha urged.

"There are small variations in the story, but they reflect the original. When the Magi went to visit the Christ child they stopped at an old lady's home. She was famous for keeping the cleanest home in the land because she was constantly sweeping. They stayed with her for a day, resting themselves and their animals. When they left they invited her to go with them to see the Christ child. Befana told them she couldn't because she had too much housework to do. They left. A few hours later she changed her mind and set out after them, taking a present with her for the child. She flew on her broom trying to find them or the Christ child, but she could not."

"That's sad," Samantha murmured.

"It was, but she dedicated herself from that time forward to the Christ child. Every year on the night before Epiphany she visits all the children in Italy and leaves them gifts in their stockings since she was unable to give a gift to Jesus. If they were good she leaves them fruit, sweets, or toys. If they were bad she leaves them a lump of coal or a stick. Although these days it tends to be candy that looks like coal so that even the naughty children get something."

"So, like Santa Claus," Samantha said.

"Yes, only Befana did this in Italy long before the man in the red suit."

"That explains some of the witch decorations I saw up in some of the stores."

"Yes. This town is very special because it is said to be the home of Befana. Every year they have a festival in her honor and build her a house and deliver letters to her from children all over the country."

"It's a wonderful story," Samantha said, still trying to work out what it was Sofia's grandmother wanted.

"It would be, if it was a story. It's not, though. It's history. My family's history, to be exact."

"I don't understand."

"My ancestor was that woman who welcomed the Magi into her home and then tried too late to find the baby. She spent the rest of her life proclaiming the coming of the Christ child and leaving treats for children. When she died, her daughter kept up the tradition. And her daughter after her, and so forth."

"Your Grandmother is the current Befana," Samantha realized.

"Yes. And had my parents not been killed in a car accident when I was little my mother would have taken over from her years ago."

"But instead she's looking to you to become the next Befana."

"She is, and I don't want to do it," Sofia said miserably. "All my life it has been planned for me. This is what I'm to do. No choice, no ability to make a different life for myself."

Sofia didn't want to work in the family business. Hers was not a new problem, but when the family business was an integral part of the way millions celebrated Christmas it became an overwhelming problem.

"Isn't there someone else who could do it? A sister, a distant cousin?"

"No, there is just me. Do you have any idea what it's like to be trapped by your own history and heritage?"

Samantha did actually. All too well.

"What is it you want to do with your life?" Samantha asked.

"I don't know. I've never even really considered it before. I didn't have to think about what I wanted to be when I grew up because that path had already been chosen for me."

"And now that it's here you're scared."

"It's more than that. I can't be Befana. I'm nothing like the women of my family. I'm a good Christian; I just have never really felt the Christmas spirit in my heart."

"Maybe that's because you've always felt the coming burden of being a cultural icon. And I don't know about your grandmother or her mother, but you sound just like that first woman. You're too busy worrying about the job you have to do in order to see the magic and the wonder that is calling out to you."

Sofia shuddered at Samantha's words. "You're right, I am like her," she said, tears beginning to fall freely.

Samantha let the other woman cry for a couple of minutes before she said, "Maybe you should learn from her and find the joy before it's too late."

"What if I'm not as good at being Befana as my grandmother and all the others?"

Sofia was sinking downward in a spiral of fear and despair. Samantha touched her arm again and this time she sent an electrical shock through her.

"Ouch!" Sofia exclaimed. "What did you do that for?"

"I needed to make sure I had your full attention. You don't have to be as good as any of the other Befanas. You just have to do the best job you can. That's all God asks of you, and we can't hold ourselves to a higher standard than He does."

"Do you really believe that?"

"I do. With all my heart."

"You would make a good Befana," Sofia said.

Samantha smiled. "It might be in my heart, but it's not in my blood."

"I just wish I knew everything was going to be okay," Sofia said.

"I might be able to help with that," Samantha said, remembering the pearl necklace she had been keeping on her so that it didn't fall into the wrong hands. Moments later she held it out to Sofia.

"The pearl is magic," Samantha said. "It helps you find your destiny."

Sofia hesitated, but finally reached out and touched it. A moment later her face lit up with the happiest glow.

Sofia reached out and hugged her. "Thank you," she whispered.

"I take it you liked what you saw?"

"You were right. I just have to be the best Befana I can be."

A moment later Sofia pulled away and started to hand the pearl back to Samantha.

"No, I think you should keep it," Samantha told her. "It's my Christmas present to you."

"I can never repay you."

"Just make all those children happy," Samantha said with a smile.

Sofia nodded as she put the necklace on. After a few minutes they stood up to walk back to Sofia's house.

"So, you must be going to be one of the youngest Befanas," Samantha said.

"There have been a few younger."

"Yet she's depicted as an old woman."

Sofia laughed and passed a hand over her face. When she turned and looked at Samantha she looked just like an old crone. The glamour she had thrown was almost perfect. Even Samantha could barely tell that what she was seeing was only illusion.

Sofia had been right about one thing, the town really knew how to throw a fun festival. Samantha had been spending all morning walking around with her loved ones and enjoying all the festivities.

At last the time came when Befana was presented the little house that had been constructed for her for the holiday.

"You're sure that's really a young woman?" her father asked as he stared at what seemed to be a very old woman dressed in black and carrying a broomstick.

Samantha was staring past the glamour and what she saw made her heart sing. "Yes, it is a young woman, and a very happy one at that."

Christmas Glamour

Fifteen Years From Now

Sometimes Miranda Matthews hated her day job. As a crime scene photographer she got to see man's inhumanity to man close up and yet was powerless to do anything about it. Unfortunately her day job was a necessary evil, the way she hid what she truly was beneath a conforming exterior. Truth was she was a woman with at least one too many identities. Her day job might have Miranda Matthews taking pictures of bodies and horrific crimes, but her night job, that of the superhero Glamour, had her stopping crime and saving people.

Of course, as her father was overly fond of telling her, neither of those jobs was her *real* job. Or even her real name for that matter. She was Miranda Merlin, descendant of the wizard Merlin, and part of the family Merlin who throughout history guided and protected Arthur whenever he would appear again to save the people. And of all the Merlin family members currently living, Miranda just happened to be The Merlin, the one true advisor to the Once and Future King. She had gained that title by being the first of the Merlin family to come across Arthur in his current form.

The only problem was, she hadn't managed to figure out who Arthur actually was. She had a list of eight men, all of whom possessed the requisite courage and skills, all of whom were in her life in one way or another. And it wasn't like she could just casually try to ask them in conversation if they were the only hope for the current generation. Unlike Merlins, Arthurs had no idea who they were until they were united with both Merlin and Excalibur. The worst part was, the sword wasn't even in her possession. An entire different family served as the sword keepers, known as Stones. It was the current Stone's job to seek out Arthur and test him to see if he was ready and worthy to wield the ancient sword. The current Stone was quite devoted to his job and quite stubborn. He was throwing challenges at all eight men constantly leaving her running around trying to watch and help each of them. The man didn't even have the courtesy to let her know which men he was testing when. Yet even still, she hated her day job worse than her "real job".

"Matthews, you okay?" Detective David Vaughn asked her.

She looked up at him. David was her boyfriend. Not that anyone knew that. Interoffice romances were an official no-no and as much as she hated her day job she still needed it. Surprisingly there was no money in being a superhero or being the wizard meant to shepherd a king. She wished she could tell David the truth. She wished she could unburden herself on him, but she couldn't.

David didn't know about either of her other jobs. The Merlin one was getting particularly difficult to hide from him, though, given that he was one of the eight men who could be Arthur. *Which isn't awkward at all*, she thought in frustration.

"It's just a waste of perfectly good Christmas lights," she said, pointing to the light strand that had been used to choke the victim to death.

"Don't you mean perfectly illegal Christmas lights?"

David was right. The strand was old-fashioned, like the kind they had when she was a kid before it was illegal to have any kind of lights but white LEDs. LEDs were better for the environment and white lights were supposed to be a religious neutral color. You could celebrate Christmas, Hanukkah, Kwanza, Winter Solstice or anything else you wanted as long as other people couldn't tell by looking at your holiday display which one you were celebrating.

"It's a shame the bulbs are broken."

"Even if they weren't, it would be evidence," David said, eyeing her intently. "No sneaking it home to your secret Christmas tree."

David was taking a stab in the dark. He didn't actually know that she had a secret Christmas tree, decorated with so many different colored lights, hidden in her coat closet at home. When she got in her apartment she'd make sure all the blinds were closed before opening the door and plugging the festive decoration in. Of course it used enough of her allotment of electricity that she couldn't use the oven all month, but it was worth eating cold dinners if she could have the beautiful lights.

She shook her head slowly. The world was so messed up. Arthur needed to assume his role and fix everything. If only she could figure out who it was.

"Seriously, you okay?" David asked.

"The world is messed up. I have to do something to fix it."

He blinked at her in surprise. "Of course it's messed up, but it's not your job to fix it."

No, but it might be yours, she thought, but didn't say out loud.

By the time she had finished with what she had to do for the day Miranda was exhausted in mind and body. Every day life seemed to get harder. Either that or her tolerance was lessening. When she got home she plugged in her Christmas tree and then went to her closet. Pushing aside all the bland, colorless, environmentally friendly clothes that she, like everyone else, was required to wear she revealed her Glamour costume. Fuchsia and gold. Bright, bold, a rebellion against a grey world.

She always felt a thrill as she fingered the sleek fabric. Not tonight, though. Her heart was too heavy. Glamour had started to become an icon, a symbol, but that wasn't what the people needed. They needed a leader. And she needed help.

Twenty minutes later she was standing in her father's den and he was regarding her with suspicion.

"What do you want?" he asked.

"I want the world to be what it used to be," she admitted.

"Only Arthur can do that."

"I don't know who he is," she admitted.

"But you know who he might be."

"There are eight men that I have contact with that have the requisite courage and strength of will. The Stone has been testing all of them, but it's taking too long."

"And the testing will continue until Arthur is found. And Arthur will never be found until he knows himself. And he will never know himself until you name him."

"Yes, but there is only one true Arthur. What if I name the wrong man?"

"Then he will fail and things will become...worse."

She sat down on a chair with a sigh. "I never wanted to be The Merlin."

"I know, you would have been much happier just fighting crime and letting someone else shoulder the responsibility."

His words stung, but she didn't react.

A minute passed in silence and then her father sighed and took a seat next to her. "Being The Merlin is a great honor, and also a great burden. Each generation of our family trains, knowing they could be called, and yet they rarely are. In all the generations since the first, there has never been a Merlin family member like you. I know, I've researched. You've always been drawn to acquiring physical skills instead of mental ones. When you were three you asked me to let you learn how to fight with a sword. It was very unMerlin of you. Our minds have always been our weapons. But your gifts have always manifested themselves in different ways."

"I know, I'm the worst possible choice to be The Merlin."

"Unless you're not."

She twisted her head to see her father's face. He wasn't joking. He was serious and there was conviction in the eyes that met hers.

"What do you mean?"

"For years I tried to mold you, shape you into a normal Merlin. Maybe that's not what this world or this particular Arthur needs. I've been giving it a lot of thought and I believe there was a reason God chose you to be different. I think you are exactly who you need to be."

Tears stung her eyes. It meant everything to hear her father say that. It also helped put to rest her own doubts about her worthiness. There was something else she needed to tell him, though.

"Dad, one of the eight men...he's a man that I've been dating for a while."

"Your detective boyfriend David?"

"How did you know?" she asked.

He rolled his eyes. "Did you really think I wouldn't know something like that."

"What if...what if he's Arthur?" she asked.

"Are you worried that there's another woman out there for him or that you are the woman for him?"

"Both."

"There is not always a Guinevere. And just because you are with him doesn't mean you will become one. One of the greatest mysteries of this cyclic play we all act out is that while there are many things that always happen the same way, there are also many things that change from time to time."

"So, you're basically telling me not to worry about it?" she asked.

"I'm telling you that even though this story has played out many times before, those living through it each time are accorded a large portion of free will to fix things, make different mistakes, whatever. If your David is Arthur, don't panic. You don't yet know how the story will end for the two of you."

"Thanks."

Somewhere in the distance a chime sounded and he stood and crossed to his desk. "Your mother and I have an appointment we must keep.

I believe I have something, though, that will make your job easier. I acquired it last year."

He took a small jewelry box out of his desk drawer. He walked over and handed it to her. She opened it. Inside was a large, black pearl suspended on a simple gold chain. It had the glow of magic coming off of it.

"What is this?" she asked.

"A pearl once taken from a sea witch."

"Any relation to the Lady of the Lake?" she asked.

"A very distant cousin is my understanding. The pearl was what gave the witch her powers. It has the ability to show a person their true path, their destiny."

"I could use it to discover which man is Arthur," she realized.

"Yes. I look forward to hearing him named."

"Thank you," she said, closing the lid and putting the case in her pocket.

Miranda had a plan. It was an insane plan, but at least it was a plan. Arthur had to be found and the night the pearl came into her possession she had a dream about how she could quickly bring him forth. She hoped it wouldn't backfire on her, but what else could she do?

It was Saturday night and the man who was the current Stone was sitting in her apartment. Under his long, gray trench coat she could occasionally see the flash of metal. He had the sword Excalibur with him. When informed of her plan he had expressed neither approval or disapproval.

She had invited all eight men to her apartment for a little get-together and to her immense relief all eight had accepted. She had pulled the Christmas tree out of the closet and into the center of the room. It was the moment of truth and boldness was essential. On the tree she had hung the pearl and it reflected the lights around it making it look ethereal.

There was a knock at the door and she hurried to open it. "Hey, what's going on?" Luke, David's partner, asked as he walked inside.

"Thanks for making it, Detective," she said.

He looked at the Christmas tree and his face lit up. "Yes! Is it a secret Christmas party? I wish you'd said something, I would have brought a gift or two."

"No, not a Christmas party per se," she said.

Before she could say anything else there was a knock at the door and she turned to let a Catholic priest in. "Father Gary, thank you for making it," she said.

"I must admit, I'm curious. We met a few weeks ago, didn't we?"

"Yes, come in and have a seat."

"Father," Luke said, extending a hand.

"Detective," Gary said as he shook it.

The Stone sat silent, not introducing himself. She noted that the other two men didn't even notice him. He had a talent for fading into the background.

The twins who were both firemen and always the first responders to any emergency calls in the city arrived next followed closely by the chief coroner, an Irishman who often helped Glamour on the sly.

Thomas, her next door neighbor and an English professor with a fondness for Arthurian legends, arrived. "Sorry I'm running a couple of minutes late," he said.

"You're fine," she said, ushering him into the room.

The son of the black market meat seller that she frequented arrived next and five minutes after him David showed up at last.

"I'm not last here, am I?" he asked, hesitating as he glanced inside. He clearly wanted to kiss her, but his eyes fastened on his partner and with a sigh he walked past her. After tonight an illegal interoffice romance could easily be the least of their worries.

She closed the door and leaned against it for a moment, taking a deep breath. It was the moment of truth. One of these eight men had to be Arthur and noone was leaving until she found out which one.

She moved into the main room and stood in front of the tree. "You're probably wondering why I called you here," she said. Miranda winced, as she realized she sounded like some evil mastermind in an old film.

"What is it, Miranda?" Luke asked.

She had never told anyone her secret before and she found it quite impossible to figure out how to even start. She struggled for a moment, but the words wouldn't come. At last an idea hit her.

She took the pearl off the tree and held it up. "Before I tell you, I need each of you to hold this in your hands for a few seconds and think about your future."

"Because, that's not creepy or ominous at all," one of the twins said.

"I assure you. I have a good reason," she said and handed it to him first.

He took it, stared at it for a moment, and then clutched at his chest and fell on the ground writhing.

Several of the others jumped to their feet, but his twin just rolled his eyes and lightly kicked the fallen man who swiftly sat up with a grin.

"Sorry, couldn't help myself," he said.

Not Arthur, she thought as she took the pearl from him.

He retook his seat and she handed it to the other twin who stared thoughtfully at it for a moment before handing it back with a slight frown.

She wanted to ask him if he'd seen anything, but she hesitated. Her father hadn't told her exactly how it worked and she had touched the thing half a dozen times already without having any visions or anything herself. She'd tried to picture herself standing by Arthur's side, but even that hadn't produced any results.

"Is there something wrong?" she finally asked.

"No, just had sudden really strong thoughts about my ex-girlfriend. Kinda came out of the blue."

She nodded. It was probably safe to say that he wasn't Arthur either.

She turned to David who just shook his head. "You know I don't believe in crystal ball sort of stuff."

She fought down her irritation. She would save him for last. Hopefully they'd find Arthur before getting back around to him.

She handed the pearl to Father Gary who took it and then stared at it intently for several seconds. His eyes were actually flickering as though he was watching something unfolding before him. Finally he looked up at her. "I know that what I'm seeing is symbolic in some way."

Her heart began to pound and she found herself kneeling down in front of him. "What do you see?" she asked.

"I see myself wielding a sword."

Out of the corner of her eye she could see the Stone sit up, suddenly paying very close attention to the proceedings.

"Can you see what it looks like?" she asked.

"No, just a sword of some sort. I'm fighting a knight dressed all in green."

"The Green Knight?" Thomas, the English professor asked. "That would make you Gawain in your vision."

He was right. Gawain was the most pure-hearted of all Arthur's knights. But he was not Arthur.

"Interesting," Gary said before handing her back the pearl.

She sighed and turned toward Thomas and was startled to see how intently he was staring at her.

"You're looking for Arthur, aren't you?" he asked.

"Yes," she said.

"Arthur? What are you talking about? What's going on?" David asked.

"Arthur, King Arthur, the once and future king whose prophesied return will save his people," the professor said.

"You must be joking," David said with a derisive snort.

"Anything but. The signs are all there. And it wouldn't be the first time he'd returned if I've read my history right."

"Are you Arthur?" Miranda asked him.

Thomas reached out and wrapped his hand around hers and the pearl. "No, but since I was a very small boy I've dreamed that I was Galahad."

When he spoke the name Galahad the pearl suddenly felt like it was burning white hot in their hands.

"You are," Miranda said.

"Thank you." He squeezed her hand and then let it go.

She took a deep breath and turned to the coroner. There was open fear on the man's face as he accepted the pearl from her. He held it for only a moment and then threw it back at her with a shout.

"What's wrong?" David asked sharply.

"I saw myself dead on a slab in my own morgue," the man said his voice shaking.

She took a shaky breath, not wanting to think of him that way. At least she knew he wasn't Arthur.

She turned to the meat seller's son and he reached out with a large hand that was steady as a rock. He took the pearl from her and squeezed it tight. He closed his eyes for a moment and when he opened them there was a look of wonder in his eyes.

"Are you Arthur?" she breathed.

"No, I serve Merlin," he said.

"Merlin, right, and exactly who is that supposed to be?" David asked.

"It's Miranda, you idiot," Thomas said, sarcasm thick in his voice.

David started up out of his chair and she threw up a hand. "Sit back down!" she barked. He did as he was told.

That left him and Luke. She handed the pearl to Luke who took it almost reverently from her hand. He held it for a moment and then looked at her, excitement flashing across his face.

"You're Glamour, the superhero!" he said.

She felt herself flush as she snatched the pearl away from him. Luke was an admirer of Glamour's. David, her boyfriend, was not.

As she turned to David he stared at her in disbelief. "You?" he asked.

"Yes, now, please take the pearl and tell me if you're Arthur," she said, handing it to him.

It had to be. He was the last one and she knew that one of these men was the one she was searching for.

He took the pearl from her and there was a look of anger and betrayal on his face that startled her. She knew he didn't approve of Glamour, but she had not expected him to react quite so negatively to finding out it was her.

"You know what I see?" he asked her.

"What?"

"I see myself walking out of here and forgetting all this nonsense," he said.

He dropped the pearl on the floor and stood up.

She snatched the pearl up off the ground and confronted him. "You have to be Arthur, there's noone else."

He stared at her like she'd lost her mind and she was beginning to feel like she had.

Slowly Luke stood to his feet. "You didn't let me finish," he said softly.

She turned to look at him and so did David.

"I saw you, Glamour, Merlin, and you were putting a crown upon my head after I took Excalibur from the little gray man in the corner."

He pointed to the Stone and everyone else turned to look. She heard a couple of the men gasp and Gary stood to his feet. "Where did he come from?" he asked.

"He's been here the entire time we have been," Luke said. "Did none of the rest of you see him?"

"None of the rest of them were worthy to take Excalibur from me," the Stone said as he stood and walked forward. He pulled the jeweled sword from inside his coat and extended the hilt toward Luke.

"You all are nuts," David said. He turned, and just like he had foreseen, he left the apartment without looking back. Miranda's heart constricted, but she had to let him go. What was happening now was bigger than both of them and she had to stay and see this through.

"Only he who would be king, he who is Arthur, may take this sword from my hands," the Stone said.

Luke reached out and grasped the hilt. He pulled the sword toward him and it left the Stone's hands. Luke held it high and the reflection of the Christmas tree lights danced along the blade giving it an unearthly glow. The remaining men sank to their knees and bowed their heads, acknowledging their rightful leader.

Miranda stared at Luke and whispered, "Hail, Arthur, the once and future king."

The Kiss of Christmas Future

"And my spirit hath rejoiced in God my Saviour."

- Luke 1:47

France, Thirty Years From Now

The Savior. It's all about the Savior.

It was Christmas and all around Gabriel people were celebrating the Christ child born in the stable. When he thought of the Savior, though, he never pictured him as a child. He pictured him as a grown man, hanging on a cross, covered in blood and death hovering upon him. The ultimate sacrifice for the redemption of mankind.

He had never had a child in the human sense of it. Maybe that was why he couldn't relate to the adoration of the infant. But he was in humble awe of the man who had chosen pain and degradation and ultimately given his life for all, including him and his kind. Sometimes being unable to truly see his Christ as a baby made him feel apart from the rest of humanity. That was okay. Gabriel was used to being alone.

Most of the time he preferred it that way, but even he had to admit that at Christmas he found himself longing for those he had once known who no longer walked the earth. His thoughts turned as they so often did to his beloved Carissa. No one had celebrated Christmas with more joy and abandon than her. Every year she would challenge him to decorate the entire castle before she could finish decorating a single room. Every year she lost due to his vampiric speed, but it never kept her from trying to beat him.

He glanced down at the invitation in his hand. He wasn't sure how David and Wendy had even known where to send it to. He hadn't seen them for three decades. It seemed they were throwing a Christmas party that was also going to be a celebration of the graduation of their son, Paul, from seminary.

He stared at the engraved paper, wondering if they had invited his sire to the party as well. Paul was the vampire who had turned him and had been a monk for nearly two millennia now. He did not doubt that David and Wendy had named their son in honor of him. After all, Paul was the one who had been tasked with training David to fight vampires so that he might survive the war that had been thrust upon them all.

"I'm not going," Gabriel said to the dog that was lying on the stone floor next to him, gazing into the heart of the fire.

The animal looked up, wicked fangs flashing in the firelight. The dog was a vampire and therefore immortal. It was unnatural, a monstrosity for an animal to be turned. His sire had been one of the Raiders who had once dogged Susan and Raphael's footsteps. The dog had been freed from the control of that master when he was killed. He had retreated to the forest for a while where Gabriel had eventually found him.

He had named the Gaston, after one of his favorite pets from centuries before. This one wasn't as smart or as beautiful as his old dog had been, but had the distinct advantage of being the one creature he could share eternity with.

Gabriel reached down and scratched behind the dog's ears. "No, definitely not going," he told the animal.

Gaston thumped his tail on the floor, enjoying the attention.

Still, though, there was a nagging question in the back of his mind. Why had they reached out after so many years?

Gaston whined and stood to his feet, staring intently at the door that led out into the hall. Gabriel strained, listening for whatever it was that had caught the animal's attention.

At last he was rewarded with the sound of a soft click. Someone had entered his home. He rose in expectation of the visitor who appeared moments later in the doorway.

"Paul," Gabriel said, acknowledging his sire.

The monk smiled at him as he strode forward. "Gabriel, it has been too long."

Gabriel lifted the invitation he was still holding. "Something tells me that you're here because of this party that David and Wendy are throwing."

"You are, of course, correct," Paul said, pausing to scratch Gaston under the chin.

"Do you know why they've invited us?"

"No. I'm as much in the dark as you."

"And yet you knew I would be receiving an invitation as well."

Paul shrugged. "I saw it in a dream."

"So you are going?"

"I am."

"Have you ever even been to the New World?" Gabriel asked.

"It's been settled for many centuries. I don't think it can properly be called the 'new world' anymore," Paul said.

"Everything is relative," Gabriel countered.

"No, I have not been to the Americas, though I have been meaning to go for some time."

"I'm not sure you'll like California."

"I understand this time of the year there isn't nearly the hours of daylight that there are the rest of the year."

"I was talking about the culture."

"And I was trying to ignore what you were talking about."

Gabriel rolled his eyes. "You're going then?"

"Yes, and I think you should, too."

"Why?"

"Because they asked."

"So?"

Paul narrowed his eyes. "Have they asked anything of you in thirty years?"

"No."

"That's why."

Gabriel sighed and glanced at Gaston. "Well, boy, it looks like we're going after all."

"It's chaos," Paul muttered as he stared out the window of the car as Gabriel drove across the Golden Gate Bridge in San Francisco. "Beautiful, but complete chaos."

There were so many lights that Gabriel was having to squint to block out some of the light. There was so much of it that it was actually painful to his vampire senses. In the back seat Gaston was pacing restlessly. It had been simple to mesmerize a handful of people so that they didn't notice that the dog had taken up a seat of his own on the flight. Riding in the cargo hold couldn't have hurt the dog, but Gabriel had been afraid of what Gaston might have done once night fell and he woke up. There was no cage known to man that could have held the animal for more than a second.

"I don't know how so many of these drivers are managing not to get into an accident with their human reflexes," Paul noted as Gabriel executed a swift lane change to avoid being sideswiped.

"It is a mystery."

Once they had made it across the bridge traffic evened out a bit. It was still heavy, but Gabriel was able to weave in and out, speeding past the other cars. His enhanced reflexes made it easy and his keen vision spotted the two police cars on the road long before they ever saw him. It wasn't long before they were pulling up to a house on the outskirts of Novato that was sitting on a couple of acres of land, isolated from its neighbors.

It was probably just as well. Close neighbors might have complained about the staggering number of Christmas lights adorning the house.

"I bet they can see this place from space," Paul muttered as he put a hand up to shield his eyes.

Carissa would have loved it. It seemed Wendy shared something of her ancestor's spirit as well as her looks.

They got out of the car and walked to the door. Before they reached it an older man threw it open wide.

"Friends, come in," he boomed in a rich voice.

Gabriel blinked as he recognized David, now thirty years older. That was one of the strangest things about knowing mortals - watching them age. It never ceased to amaze him. David's hair was gray at his temples and his once smooth face now bore several lines in it.

Gabriel and Paul walked inside and David closed the door behind them. The house was large, roomy, but comfortable looking. Everywhere he looked were the trappings of

Christmas. It seemed there were nearly as many lights inside as there had been outside. He could see through into the dining room where a couple people were sitting. Wendy had stood up and came out to greet them.

"It's so good to see you both," she said warmly as she stopped in front of them.

"How are you?" Paul asked.

"I'm good, and you?"

"Fine," Paul said.

Wendy, however, wasn't. She was sick. Gabriel could smell the difference in her body chemistry, something that would have been undetectable to a normal human. He didn't have to smell the sickness to know, though. She was pale and her face drawn. Carissa had looked like that toward the end of her life. Wendy had always closely resembled Carissa, but never more so than now.

"How long are the doctors giving you?" he asked.

She blinked in surprise and then hastily glanced over her shoulder. When she looked back at him she looked older, strained. "We can discuss that later," she said softly.

Her son didn't know.

"For now," she said with a pained smile, "it's time Paul meets his namesake."

She led the way into the dining room. "Paul, I'd like you to meet the man we named you after. Brother Paul, this is our son," she said, making the introductions.

Paul had risen from the table. Gabriel noticed with a pang how much he looked like his mother. If Carissa had lived a different life she might have had a son that looked like him.

The two Pauls shook hands.

"From what my parents have told me about you, I had expected you to be a much older man," the boy said.

Paul glanced at David who was almost imperceptibly shaking his head.

"What can I say? I've aged well," the monk said drily.

Gabriel barely contained a smirk.

"And this is Gabriel," Wendy said.

"It's a pleasure," the boy said.

He wasn't technically a boy. He looked to be about twenty-two or twenty-three, but relatively speaking he seemed a mere child. Another of the hazards of living forever. It was sometimes hard to view people as adults rather than children.

"And this is his friend and partner-in-crime, Will," David said, introducing the other boy.

"Pleased to meet you," Will said. "Interesting looking dog you've got there."

"Don't touch the dog," Gabriel said, impressing that thought on all the humans present. One by one each of them nodded.

"I hate to run, but we're meeting some of our classmates tonight for a pre-graduation celebration," young Paul said after a minute.

"Just be careful," Wendy said.

"Of course," Will said with a grin as the two boys left.

Once they were gone Wendy turned to the two vampires with a look of distress on her face.

"We can talk now," she said.

"What's wrong?" Gabriel asked. "I noticed that he didn't seem to be aware that we were vampires."

"Unfortunately, we made a mistake with Paul," David said grimly.

"We didn't want him growing up afraid, looking over his shoulder all the time," Wendy said.

"You didn't tell him about vampires," Gabriel guessed.

"No. When he was seventeen we decided it was time to tell him."

"And he didn't believe you?" Paul asked.

"No."

Gabriel frowned. "Surely Raphael could have shown him the truth."

"He was less than eager to help in that regard," Wendy said with a sigh. "So, after a while we dropped it. After all, tens of millions of people go about their lives never knowing the truth. We thought maybe he'd be better off, that maybe he was meant to live a normal life."

"But something changed?" Gabriel guessed.

"We think he's somehow acquired a stalker. One that only comes out at night."

"The two of you should be more than a match for an ordinary vampire at this point," Paul said.

"That's just it. She never gets near enough for us to even get a good sense of her," David said with a frustrated sigh.

"Let alone put a stake in her," Wendy added.

"And you can't talk to your son about it because he'll just think you're crazy."

They nodded, clearly distressed by the whole situation.

"Are you wanting us to stop her or enlighten him?"

"Both," David said emphatically. "It was foolish of us to think that our son could go through life without attracting this kind of attention. People in this family don't really get a choice about that."

David was right about that, Gabriel thought grimly.

"We'll do what we can," Paul said.

"That's all we can ask," David said.

"We'll talk to him when he comes home tonight," Paul said.

"Excellent. I can show you your rooms now," David said.

"There will be time for that later. First, Wendy, my child, what is wrong with you?" Paul asked.

"Cancer. It's everywhere. At the rate she's going downhill it won't be long, so we've been told," David said with a catch in his voice.

"And your son doesn't know that either."

"We didn't want to ruin his graduation or Christmas. We figured we'd wait until after the holidays to tell him."

It was a mistake, but it was theirs to make.

They visited for a couple of hours. Gaston had made himself comfortable in front of the fireplace. Finally Wendy and David excused themselves to go to bed. Gabriel and Paul sat staring at the fire.

"You figured out how you want to handle the boy?" Gabriel asked after a while.

"No, although I have a feeling subtle won't work on him from what his parents said."

"Given that he might have a stalker and that he is completely unprepared for any of this, we can't be warm and fuzzy. We need to put the fear of God in him, so to speak."

"Agreed. Let's just try not to break him in half while we're doing it," Paul said, a light dusting of sarcasm in his voice.

"Name one person I've broken in half."

"I can name an entire village in Africa where you broke everyone in half."

Gabriel sighed. "You have a cursed good memory."

"What good's being cursed with immortality if you can't remember the past and learn from it?"

Gaston lifted his head and glanced toward the door, then yawned and flipped to his other side.

A few seconds later Gabriel heard the car coming.

By the time the car had pulled up outside, Will had dropped off Paul, and driven away nearly five minutes had passed. A few seconds later young Paul came through the front door, jumping a little when he saw them staring at him.

"My folks asleep?" he asked as he closed and locked the door.

"Yes. Did you have fun with your friends?" Paul asked, voice pleasant.

"Yes. I would have figured you'd be asleep after your long flights."

"Well, you know, we wanted to talk, get a chance to get acquainted finally," the monk said.

"That's very thoughtful. It's getting late, though, and you'll be here for a few days-"

"Sit down," Gabriel interrupted, putting enough force into his voice to ensure that the young man hastily sat down on a chair facing them.

"You know, we're very *old* friends of your parents," the monk said. "There's a reason we look this young. One your parents tried to talk to you about a few years ago."

"What are you talking about?" the boy asked.

"Vampires," the monk said bluntly. "We're talking about vampires."

The boy actually rolled his eyes. "Not you, too. Look, I know my parents believe some crazy stuff. Took me a while to try and forget it. I thought they were really cracking up. They haven't talked about that for years, though."

"Because you weren't ready to hear the truth. Vampires exist. You're talking to two of them." The monk bared his teeth, exposing his wickedly long fangs. They were longer even than Gabriel's. The length of a vampire's fangs was relative to its age.

"Look, I don't know what you're trying to pull. But it's not funny."

"Good, because we're not joking," Gabriel growled. He rose and a moment later had hoisted Paul high into the air. The boy screamed and stared down at him, clawing at his arm. Gabriel made sure he got a good look at his fangs and he snarled, knowing that when his face contorted he looked demonic.

Look at me! he commanded, reaching inside the young man's mind.

"I can hear you, in my head," he gasped.

That's right. And I'm going to stay in your head until you're ready to listen, Gabriel responded. *This is not a game, not a fantasy. This is life and death and you are in serious trouble.*

"Mom, Dad!" the boy shouted.

"They won't help you," the older Paul said, voice still calm. "They wanted us to talk to you, straighten you out about a few things."

"Please, don't hurt me!"

Coward. Your father is twice the man you'll ever be, Gabriel said, pushing deeper into the boy's mind.

And he could tell he struck a nerve. The boy actually jerked.

"I think you can put him down now, Gabriel," his sire said.

"Not sure if he's ready to listen," Gabriel growled.

"I am! I'll listen!" the boy promised.

"That's good. Listening is an essential skill for those who go into ministry," the monk said.

Gabriel considered just dropping him, but finally set him back on his chair. Then he resumed his own seat on the couch with lightning speed.

"You...you didn't move. How are you over there? What, what?" the boy panted.

"Let's try this again," the elder Paul said. "The word you are looking for is vampire."

Gabriel could sense Wendy and David upstairs. Their son's cries had roused them. *Sleep, all will be well*, he told each of them. And to their credit, even though it had been decades since he had spoken inside their heads they recognized his voice immediately and went back to sleep.

By the time the night was coming to a close young Paul had gone through denial, shock, and had arrived at acceptance tinged with awe. Perhaps most interesting to him was the news that Raphael was a vampire as well. It seemed to explain some mixed feelings he'd had for years about his uncle.

When Wendy and David came downstairs their son was exhausted, but calm. He immediately rose, hugged both his parents, and apologized to them for thinking they had been crazy.

"Have you talked about the girl yet?" David asked, wiping his eyes after hugging his son.

"What girl?" young Paul asked.

"Your parents tell us you have a stalker that only comes out at night."

"Oh, Dahlia? Yeah, she's a bit creepy. Wait, are you saying she's a vampire?" he asked, eyes widening.

"That's what we're going to find out," Gabriel said.

"And I'll give you a crash course in self defense," the monk said.

"He's the one who taught me. No one finer," David said.

"So, where we can find this Dahlia?" Gabriel asked.

"I don't know," the boy said. "I met her a few months ago at a party at a friend of a friend's house. She kinda creeped me out, but she started popping up at different places that I went."

"Would the friend of the friend whose party it was know how to get hold of her?"

"No. I asked around. No one had ever seen her before. No one knows anything about her."

"We'll soon fix that. Do you have any idea where she's going to show up next?"

"She sent me a voicemail saying that she wasn't going to miss seeing me graduate. I tried calling the phone back, but it was already disconnected."

"If she's there, we'll find her, and one way or another we'll put a stop to this," Gabriel promised.

"You should get some sleep," Wendy told her son.

"I don't know how, but I'll try." He headed upstairs, leaving the four of them alone.

"The rooms in the basement should be comfortable. Your doors lock from the inside so you control access and they are free of windows," David said. "I can't thank you enough for helping."

Yet Gabriel could tell that there was more. The sun would be up in just a few minutes, but he could sense the urgency that David was feeling. It was making even him jumpy.

"You want something else," he finally said.

David and Wendy exchanged a quick look.

"There was another reason why we asked Paul here specifically," David said.

"Something more you want me to do for your son?" the monk asked.

"No, something you can do for me," Wendy said, face pale.

"What is it you're wanting from me?" Paul asked Wendy, forehead creasing as he frowned.

"Isn't it obvious?" she asked.

The monk shook his head.

"I know who you are...who you were. I know that through you God has performed signs and wonders."

"I still don't understand," Paul said.

"Because you don't want to hear what she's saying," Gabriel broke in. "She wants you to lay hands on her and pray for her healing."

Paul looked startled. "I can't. I don't do that...anymore."

"Was that God's choice or yours?" Wendy asked pointedly.

He paused and Gabriel could feel the conflicting emotions in his mentor. The man wasn't doing a good job of keeping them in check and they were as easy for Gabriel to read as a book would be.

"I'm a monk now. Not an evangelist."

"And has a monk never performed a miracle?" Wendy challenged.

Paul's lips tightened. "When they do they get a lot more attention than they bargained for."

"That's due to continuous effort and people spreading the word," David said. "We're not asking you to call on God to perform an hundred miracles. Just one."

"We will tell no one that you were involved," Wendy said.

Paul turned to Gabriel and his eyes looked like those of a trapped and frightened animal. "Tell them I can't," he said, voice brimming with anger.

"Are you afraid God won't answer your prayers as He once did?" Gabriel asked calmly.

Paul actually bared his teeth at him. "I wouldn't expect that, coming from you."

"Why not? You're the one who spent centuries telling me not to run from God."

Paul's face twisted in rage and for a moment Gabriel thought he was actually going to try and attack him. He had only ever seen his sire lose control once, and it had not been a pretty thing. It was certainly something David and Wendy didn't need to witness.

He reached out and placed his hand on the monk's shoulder. "Steady," he urged, dropping his voice and willing Paul to listen to him.

"You know that doesn't work on me," Paul said. His voice was calmer, though, and his eyes were clearing of the hate that had been shining in them.

Gabriel gave him a small smile and Paul nodded at last as his posture relaxed.

"I think I'm more afraid that God will answer my prayers," Paul admitted.

Because then you'd have to acknowledge that it was you and not God that chose for you to go into isolation? Gabriel asked him silently, placing his thoughts in the other's mind.

Yes, Paul admitted silently.

"Don't you think either way you need to know the answer?" Gabriel said, speaking out loud again. "Even if you don't, you owe it to Wendy to try. She fought and sacrificed as much as anyone.

DEBBIE VIGUIÉ

More even than her cousin in the years after Prague."

"You're right. I owe it to Wendy, and I owe it to myself," Paul said. "You'd better sit down."

Wendy sat on the couch and David sat down beside her, slinging a protective arm around her. Paul stepped forward and placed his hand on her forehead. He closed his eyes and lifted his head toward heaven.

"Father God, we praise You in the highest. Hear our prayers and heal this, Your daughter, who has given much in Your service. In Your love and mercy, strike the cancer from her for Your glory. Amen."

Paul dropped his hand and moved swiftly back. On the couch Wendy reeled slightly and David kept her upright. She pressed her hand to her chest. "It worked. I can feel it!" she gasped.

"She's right. The smell of sickness has suddenly left her," Gabriel affirmed. He was not surprised, but it was still startling. One moment she was dying and the next she wasn't.

He turned and looked at Paul. The monk was staring, eyes wide. Gabriel could tell that he had truly not believed that she would be healed.

"Makes you think, doesn't it?" he whispered so softly that only the other vampire could hear him.

Paul faintly nodded.

123

They were lucky that the graduation ceremonies were at night. They were being held in the auditorium of the seminary. Paul was with his classmates getting ready. Wendy and David were with their guests taking their places in the audience. Gabriel and the vampire Paul were patrolling the outside of the building looking for a young woman with black hair tipped with blue dressed all in black.

Gabriel thought she sounded more like a confused Goth girl than a vampire from her description. Still, they weren't taking any chances. Everyone in the know was armed to the teeth with stakes and holy water.

With only fifteen minutes until the ceremony was set to start, Gabriel was patrolling the back entrance to the building while Paul was stationed at the front. They were keeping up a complete mental conversation as they did. After much debate they had left Gaston back at the house. The vampire dog would add a level of chaos they didn't need to deal with even though his senses would have come in handy.

As it turned out, they didn't need him, because Gabriel spotted Dahlia coming a long ways off. He melted into the shadows, letting Paul know he had seen her. He waited as she approached the back door of the building. Even though she was dressed like a Goth her movements were so swift that he instantly revised his opinion.

She was definitely a vampire.

She was nearly at the door when he flashed out of the shadows, grabbed her, threw her against the wall and pinned her there with a stake tip just piercing her chest.

She cried out in terror and he got a good look at her fangs. She wasn't that old. Maybe fifty years a vampire. Which meant she was probably coming out of the initial animalistic phase and was confused and trying to control what was happening to her.

"Where is your sire?" he demanded.

"Dead," she bleated. "I think. Years ago."

She was terrified. She was also so lost it was pitiful. Given her age it was possible she had been one of the humans turned solely for the purpose of creating a vampire army for the war that had been fought thirty years before.

His own sire was at his side in a moment. "What is your interest in the boy?" he demanded.

"He's special. I don't know why, I can just feel it."

"You need to leave him alone," Gabriel said, putting all his force into bending her will to his.

Her face contorted. "I...can't..." she wailed at last. "We're going to be together...I'm going to make him like me."

Before Gabriel could respond Paul had grabbed his hand and driven the stake it was holding into her. She collapsed in a pile of dust.

"She was beyond saving, one of the broken ones that monster created," he said softly. "Only a broken one would ever think of cursing an innocent in the way they had been cursed."

The monk was right. Gabriel was just use to Paul showing more mercy and understanding than he was. There was no doubt, though. Her own words had condemned her.

"Shall we go inside now? I don't want to miss this," the monk said.

Gabriel was able to communicate briefly to Wendy, David, and their son that the threat was over. There'd be time enough for explanations later.

The graduation ceremony itself was simple and elegant. Afterward everyone headed back to the house and tables were loaded with food and presents. The graduate was walking around, shaking hands and beaming.

At last he came to them. Before he could say anything, Paul handed him a small box. The younger Paul opened it to reveal a tie tack set with a massive black pearl. Gabriel was close enough that he could feel a faint shimmer of magic coming off the pearl itself. He had no idea where his sire had come across it.

"A pearl tie tack?" the young man asked.

"Not just any pearl. This one is magic. It's supposed to help you find and understand your destiny," the monk said with a gentle smile.

"Really?"

"That's what I've heard. It's up to you to find out."

"Thank you. For everything," the young man said. He looked at both of them. "I will never forget what you taught me."

"Good," Gabriel said.

The boy spontaneously hugged the monk and after a surprised moment Paul hugged him back. When they broke away the young Paul turned to Gabriel. "I'm sorry, but you scare me too much to hug you."

Gabriel permitted himself to smile, making sure the other got an eyeful of his fangs. "I appreciate that."

The boy shuddered slightly, but kept smiling. He nodded his head and then turned to go greet some of the others who had come to wish him well.

"He's going to be okay," Gabriel said.

"He's not the one I'm worried about."

"Oh?" he turned to his sire with a frown.

"I think the pearl worked some of its magic on me," Paul said with a sigh.

"How so?" Gabriel asked.

"You were right. I was afraid of finding out the truth. It wasn't God who wanted me to lock myself away in a monastery. It was me. I was frightened of myself back in those days, struggled with guilt over the things I had done both before and after I was turned."

"Now that you know that?"

"He's made it clear He wants me to walk among His sheep again."

"They are sorely in need of a shepherd to guide them," Gabriel said.

"And as long as I am only guiding them and not controlling them, forcing them on the path, then I am doing God's work in a way that is glorifying to Him."

"I know of no one better qualified. There's just one problem."

"What's that?" Paul asked.

"You're going to have to figure out if you're Catholic or Protestant. If you're Protestant there's many different denominations to choose from. You might want to do a little research before leaving the monastery behind to walk among the people."

"Christ came to remove barriers, not erect them."

Gabriel smiled faintly. "Then as one spreading His word, perhaps you should do the same."

"When did you get so wise?"

"A long time ago. You're just finally noticing." Gabriel looked around at the happy, smiling people. Most were strangers, but a few he realized were very dear to him even though it had been so long since they had been in his life. Then he heard himself suggesting, "Let's stay a few more days. We have nowhere we have to go, and it might be nice to spend Christmas with family for once."

DEBBIE VIGUIÉ

Debbie Viguié is the New York Times Bestselling author of more than two dozen novels including the *Wicked* series, the *Crusade* series and the *Wolf Springs Chronicles* series co-authored with Nancy Holder. Debbie also writes thrillers including *The Psalm 23 Mysteries,* the *Kiss* trilogy, and the *Witch Hunt* trilogy. When Debbie isn't busy writing she enjoys spending time with her husband, Scott, visiting theme parks. They live in Florida with their cat, Schrödinger.

Manufactured by Amazon.ca
Acheson, AB